Trumpets in the Morning

ZONDERVAN HEARTH BOOKS
Available from your Christian Bookseller

A HEARTH ROMANCE

Trumpets in the Morning

Lon Woodrum

ZONDERVAN
PUBLISHING HOUSE

OF THE ZONDERVAN CORPORATION | GRAND RAPIDS, MICHIGAN 49506

There is a legend that when Satan was roaming the universe he met Michael the Archangel, and the latter asked Satan what he missed most in heaven. Satan said, "Most of all I miss the trumpets in the morning!"

TRUMPETS IN THE MORNING

Copyright 1960 by Zondervan Publishing House
Grand Rapids, Michigan

First printing of paperback edition   1970
Seventh printing   1978

ISBN 0-310-34782-3

Printed in the United States of America

PROLOGUE

Since midafternoon nature had been setting the stage for a tragedy in Sheola.

The people of Sheola, depressed by humidity, had glanced into the brassy sky, hearing the sound overhead, a rumbling as if giant stage hands prepared for the dreadful drama.

Thunder-crags had thickened in the sky as night came on; the sultry heat had intensified. A mighty column of cold air thrust downward, colliding with a column of hot air that rushed upward. Another draft of cold air poured in from the northeast and arrowed through the mattress of hot air, shooting like a spear earthward, drilling a hole as it fell; and the column of hot air rushed wildly up the hole, screaming like a thousand sirens, climbing up and up, creating a funnel as it rose. It shuddered and climbed on upward, faster and faster, until it reached three hundred miles an hour, four hundred.

The vast funnel twisted like a giant snake, dropping earthward with its deafening doom-sound. It struck the ground at the edge of Sheola and a grain elevator came apart like a jug shattering. It hit a powerline and turned it to threads spraying in the wind of a titanic electric fan, rushing into the awful wind-column, crackling like the big guns on a man-of-war.

The wind struck a car and ripped away the glass windows, leaving the car standing there. It found a man and sucked the air from his lungs until they collapsed like a punctured toy balloon. It moved on into Sheola, zig-zagging, doing its death-dance, sounding like a hundred express trains rushing on a central target.

Near the downtown area of Sheola stood a brick and stone structure known as Christ Church.

The church stood in the path of the tornado.

A man sat in the church study with his memories. A drama ran across his mind; a drama that had begun on a day last March; and it was now the first day of September.

CHAPTER 1

IT WAS THE LAST DAY OF MARCH. He finished writing a letter on his typewriter and scrawled his name at the bottom of the page. Paul Jenner. The handwriting was almost illegible. He hoisted his six-foot length from the chair behind the broad-topped desk and moved to the window of the study.

His blue-green look ran over the part of Sheola which he could see. He could see a large part of it, for the church stood on a hill; it stood at the highest point in town, in fact. He had often reflected that this was where the church should stand, like a spiritual guardian, over the raucous, dirty oil town.

Out beyond the ragged-looking town he could see the oil derricks that speared at the sky. Out there, too, the oil-pumps were busy, day and night, jabbing their beaks into the earth. He could visualize the iron-framed oil workers, moving, joking and cursing. And at night they would bring their jokes and curses downtown and begin their drinking and fighting.

A smear of dust clung to the sky. Down in the town's streets he saw the big trucks crawling like giant beetles, making their surf-like roar.

No wonder Ann thinks the town is ugly, he thought.

He recalled how Ann had drawn back from Sheola the day they came here to pastor Christ Church.

"It almost frightens me, Paul!" she had said.

He had said, "It's not a nice-looking place. But of course I don't see it as you do. I grew up here."

"It's awfully dirty, isn't it?" she said. "It's always so clean in Grand Arbor."

His hopes that time would change Ann's attitude toward Sheola were not yet fulfilled.

Only yesterday Ann had said to him, "Paul, I get the feeling that you're not the type of man for a town like this! You're *above* it! People here won't even understand your way of preaching!"

He had shrugged and replied, "It's my business to make them understand!"

He went back to his desk and began to work on a sermon for the following Sunday morning.

He was hunting in a Concordance when he heard the sound in the doorway. He looked up to see the five-year-old boy who stood there. The boy's eyes were very blue. They searched him in an inquisitive way. The boy's hair was dark, and it was thick and curly.

"Hi, Randy," said Paul with a grin.

"Hi-ya, Daddy," said Randy. His clothes were rumpled.

"See any Indians today, pardner?" asked Paul.

Randy wagged his head soberly. "Naw."

"Any buffalo?"

"Well, maybe."

"Maybe?"

"Maybe they was only cows."

Paul nodded. "Could be, I guess."

"They could be elephants, maybe," said Randy.

"I doubt it. Not many elephants in these parts. Did you want to see me about something?"

Randy's head moved negatively. "I just wanted to look at you, I guess."

Paul rose and lifted Randy to the desk top.

"That's nice. Your wanting to look at me, I mean."

"Sure," said Randy. Then he added, "What are you doing, Daddy?"

"Working on a sermon."

Randy nodded knowingly. "I know what a sermon is."

"What?"

"A sermon is what you say that makes God seem real to people!"

Paul pursed his lips. "That's not what I told you a sermon is."

"Nonna said it."

He spread his hands. "So you like Nonna's definition of a sermon better than you like mine? Well, it's not a bad definition. That Nonna is pretty smart!"

"Nonna knows everything!" Randy said flatly.

"Now just a minute! Don't go making the lady *too* smart!"

"I like Nonna."

"Everybody likes Nonna. Well, *most* everybody."

There was another sound at the door. Paul looked up to see his wife.

"Hello, Ann." He smiled his affection.

Her eyes were even bluer than Randy's, and her hair even darker. Her carefully dressed slimness and beauty never ceased to intrigue him. Compared to his tall form she was like a child.

"Hello, Paul." Her voice reflected her quiet femininity. "I wondered what had become of Randy." There was disapproval on her delicate face. "Did you ever see anyone so dirty?"

"Dirty? I hadn't noticed."

"You hadn't *noticed?* Just look at him!"

"Just a little bit of dirt!" mumbled Randy.

A smile lighted Ann's small face as she went to Randy and hugged him closely. "Anyhow, mamma loves you."

"Sure," said Randy. "Everybody loves me!"

"Such egotism!" wailed Paul.

"What's egotism?" asked Randy.

9

"It's when your head gets too big for the rest of you, cowboy!"

Randy felt of his head. "It's not big," he muttered.

"I'd better take him home and clean him up," said Ann. "This dirty town!"

Paul lifted his shoulders and dropped them. "Any town has plenty of dirt in it for a boy to get dirty."

He went to her and slipped an arm about her slim shoulders. He stood a foot above her. "This part of the world is strange to you. But everybody can't live in Grand Arbor, Michigan, darling. Somebody has to be stuck with these oil towns."

She was silent, turning her face up, her look clinging to his. She put her slender hand on his where it rested on her shoulder. His fingers caught hers, tightened; his face was tender and protective on her.

"I'll try hard to keep this town, or anything else from hurting you, honey."

"Paul!" She put her face against his breast, holding tightly to him. "What would I ever do without you?"

He caught her to him; he lifted her face and kissed her. His mouth close to her ear, he said, "I'll always look after you, baby. You know that, don't you?"

"Yes, I know it, Paul."

"Yippee!" cried Randy, still perched on the desk. "Y-i-p-p-e-e-e!"

Ann swung toward him, her face flushing. "Oh, you!"

"You can't even be romantic around this character," wailed Paul. "Take the little barbarian home and stick him in the bath tub!"

"What's romantic?" asked Randy.

"You'll find out one day. With your looks and those eyes. Go with your mother and get the Oklahoma washed off."

"Oklahoma — I like Oklahoma."

"Oh, you'd like it anywhere," said Ann.

"Sure. Sure I like anywhere. Don't you like anywhere?"

Ann took Randy away. Paul stood grinning after them. But the grin faded presently, a small frown crept over his face.

Her unhappiness over this place keeps bothering me, he said silently.

He sat down behind his desk. He pushed a buzzer. A moment later Carla Brown came in from her office. Carla was his secretary. She was tall, finely-framed, her eyes a deep hazel. She was deeply tanned, her dress a pale blue. Her full generous mouth curved into a smile as she nodded to him.

He said, "Carla, here's the material for the bulletin next Sunday."

She took the sheaf of papers he held out. "I'm working on a sermon called 'When the Little Gods Come Down.' Like it?"

"The title, you mean?"

"Well, you couldn't very well say whether you liked the sermon — yet, could you?"

She colored slightly but he laughed. "If you don't like it, after you hear it, tell me. I value your judgment on such matters, as I've told you before."

"Thank you, Mr. Jenner." She took the papers and left.

He glanced at Ann's picture on his desk, smiling back at her smile.

I love you, his mind said to her picture.

He had seen Ann for the first time in Grand Arbor, Michigan, when he had gone there almost by accident. He had been attending Phillips University in Enid, studying for the ministry, when a friend, Peter Caldwell, whose home was in Grand Arbor, had suggested he go home with him for a Christmas weekend, and he had accepted the invitation. However, Peter, who had a father who was far from being poor, had financed the trip.

Peter Caldwell invited him to attend his home church in Grand Arbor on Sunday morning; and after the service Peter introduced him to the pastor. The latter asked Paul if he would speak to the young people's group in the evening. Paul agreed to do so. And at that meeting he saw Ann for the first time.

She was wearing a white dress, and she sat toward the front in the crowd of young people to whom Paul spoke. Her eyes were so blue that they almost seemed black at times; her young face seemed to glow against a black frame of down-combed hair that tumbled to her shoulders. The face was a sensitive delicate oval, the mouth tender and expressive. Paul found his eyes returning again and again to her face as he spoke.

Several times also his look caught on the unsmiling features of the woman who sat beside Ann. Her eyes were also blue, but much lighter than Ann's, her hair thick and gray. She was a large woman who wore an air of importance; and Paul was nagged with the feeling that she rather defied him as he spoke! The fact that she was at least fifty seemed to put her out of place among the young people.

Paul concluded his talk with, "It is not enough that we sing about the cross, or that we cling to it. We must take it up! Else we cannot be Jesus' disciples. And the cross is not an accident. It is a part of the plan of life. There is nothing big, good, worthwhile, but what at the heart of it there is a little Calvary."

Immediately after the service was dismissed Ann came to Paul.

"I'm Ann March," she said. "I really liked your talk." Her smile lighted her fragile face as a light turned on behind a window. Her eyes were very deep; they made him think of blue-black pools of water. He kept holding the slim hand she gave him until she gently withdrew it. And he flushed a little at the realization of her act.

Then the large woman with the gray hair approached them. Her very face appeared to reprimand Paul for something. Her dress was expensive, as were the jewels she wore. She did not smile when she spoke to Paul.

"I am Ann's mother," she said brusquely.

He bowed. "I'm pleased to meet you, Mrs. March."

"I always attend the young people's meeting." Her

voice seemed afraid of being silenced. "I like to know what the speakers are telling the young people."

Paul reached for a grin but it eluded him. He said quite lamely, "I hope my talk passed."

Mrs. March's lips pursed thinly. She fingered a glittering necklace with well-manicured fingers. "Must we make religion such a difficult thing? So much talk about burdens and taking up a cross! Did not Christ say that His yoke was easy?"

"Mrs. March, the cross is the symbol of the Christian faith. The cross is a thing of suffering and humiliation. How do you suppose it got on our churches?"

Mrs. March waggled her wide shoulders. "If you would be a successful minister, young man, I would suggest that you give the people something to lift them rather than a message that will depress them!"

"But, Mother, his message was not depressing," said Ann. "It was very challenging!"

"Hmmm," said her mother. "Incidentally, Mr. Jenner, I hear you are from Oklahoma. Are you in oil, your people, I mean?"

He disliked the woman at once. He said, "My father was in oil. He's dead now. As for me, you can see I'm in the ministry."

Paul kept thinking of the contrast between Ann and her mother. In Peter Caldwell's home that evening he asked him about the Marches.

"Old man March founded the March Farm Implement Company here in Grand Arbor. He made a terrific stack of money. He's dead now, but Frances March rules the old March roost with a hand of iron. She lords it over her social set, too. She's a genuine snob, believe me. Maybe you noticed her attitude."

"I could scarcely help it," said Paul. "But Ann seems nice."

"Ann is a sweet girl. Don't ask me how come. You wouldn't know the old lady was her mother. She takes after her father. He was a pretty swell guy from what I can hear.

13

His money didn't go to his head, and he was generous — when his wife didn't stymie him!''

"Ann is lovely!'' mused Paul.

"She tries to be a good Christian, too. She's humble and kind and considerate of people. Her mother, of course, tries to dominate the church and the pastor. I doubt if anyone in the church ever really thinks of her as a Christian. But they all like Ann.''

"I'd like to know Ann better,'' Paul said.

"Ha! So would a lot of young guys. I tried to know her better myself! She's not susceptible to the male charm — at least she wasn't to mine!''

That night Paul lay in bed thinking of her. Her beauty had impressed itself deeply on his mind. But a sad feeling nagged him. A girl like that, with all her money and position in society, would be out of his reach.

But the following morning as he and Peter prepared to leave for the airport Ann phoned him!

"I just wanted to wish you all the best on your trip. And to tell you again that I was impressed and challenged by your talk yesterday. I have a feeling —''

She hesitated and Paul said, "A feeling?''

"I have a feeling that you'll make a wonderful minister!'' She paused again, then said, "I wish I could hear you speak more often!''

"I wish so, too!'' he said impulsively.

"Do you?''

"Yes, I do! And maybe you will get to hear me speak often — sometime!''

"Well, I really hope so — Paul.''

That was how it began.

The courtship came back to him now as he sat in his study. He thought of the letters she had written him. He cast a look toward the bottom drawer of the desk where he kept those letters. There was a haunting poetic quality in her writing that stirred the poet that ever struggled in his own soul. And her femininity came through the letters, bright, sweet and compelling. Lines out of the letters were written in his mind.

Suddenly he pulled open the drawer and took out the bundle of letters. His name was written on the top letter. The writing was as delicate as Ann's fine face. He looked through some of the letters, smiling gently to himself. He restored the letters to the drawer.

A long breath stole into his lungs. He leaned back in his chair. More of the past tape-recorded back to him.

He was pastoring his first small charge in Oklahoma when he took a trip to Michigan to see Ann. He found her quite irresistible; and he also found her wishing to be irresistible!

The courtship was swift. The evening was unforgettable when he first held her close and told her how he loved her. She surrendered to him with a contented little cry.

"Oh, Paul! I will never stop loving you!"

Even in the sweetness of the moment a disturbing thought pricked him.

"Ann," he said, "I'm a young pastor of a small church. There's so little I can offer you. You've been used to everything that money can buy. What right have I to ask you to leave all you've known to share my place with me?"

Tears stood in her eyes. "The one real right, Paul. You said you loved me!"

Frances March received the news with an utter lack of grace. She was too angry to talk at first; and she raged in silence for two days. When she finally spoke she said bitterly, "I think Ann is a fool to marry a man with no future!"

Ann cried, "Mother, he has a wonderful future!"

"You're in love and can't think clearly, Ann," Mrs. March said. "What future has he? Very few ministers ever amounted to anything in this world!"

Paul held his peace and managed a wry grin against her wrath. "Well, there was Paul of Tarsus! He didn't do too badly. And there have been others." He was too overjoyed with his love for Ann even to feel deeply Mrs. March's insults.

"Would I want my daughter to go gadding about all over the earth with a Paul of Tarsus?" was Mrs. March's grim reply.

Paul said quietly, "I suppose not. But, Mrs. March, you must realize that Ann and I love each other. And she will be happy."

"Love!" Mrs. March grimaced. "A word for addle-headed children mostly. It takes something besides the word love to make anything a success. It takes money!"

"I'll make her happy, Mrs. March. You will see."

Ann's mother set her mouth. "Paul Jenner, listen to me. If ever you fail to treat Ann right I'll come and take her away from you! I warn you! Do you hear me?"

"Don't worry about how I'll treat Ann. She'll always be a princess to me!"

The wedding had been a massive affair. Frances March spared no expense. Having yielded to the inevitable she even pretended a vast happiness before her guests. She laughed gaily and said, "Isn't my son-in-law handsome?"

But with the wedding reception over her mien changed quickly and utterly. The face she set toward Paul was uncompromising in its opposition to him. Her angry silence gripped her once more. She locked herself in her room and refused to talk to either Ann or Paul.

Ann trembled in Paul's arms and cried, "Oh, how I wish she could understand how much we love each other!"

Frances March mellowed somewhat, outwardly at least, the next day. But her look still warned Paul that she was not his friend. A few days later Paul and Ann came to the small manse in Rimburg, Oklahoma, a bedraggled village peopled mostly by retired cotton farmers, many of whom considered the church as an organization one could join or let alone. Far too many of them decided on the latter course.

Ann and Paul were still in Rimburg when Randy was born.

CHAPTER 2

PAUL PUT AWAY HIS MEMORIES and turned back to the sermon he was working on for the following Sunday morning. His text went through his mind.

Bel boweth down; Nebo stoopeth: their idols were upon the beasts, and upon the cattle: your carriages are heavy loaden: they are a burden to the weary beast. They stoop, they bow down together; they could not deliver the burden, but themselves are gone into captivity. . . . I am God and there is none else; I am God and there is none like me. . . .

The little gods of the world, he thought, how long men have served them, and how long they have let men down! And not only ancient Bel and Nebo. There are a host of modern gods — or institutions that have replaced the gods. There are politics, money, pleasures of the flesh, even science. Little gods that finally come down because they are not big enough to be gods.

He heard the car stop outside and he went to the door. He watched the gray-haired, tall woman emerge from the Ford. She came toward him, standing straight, a dignity in the casual manner in which she carried herself.

"Hello, Nonna," he greeted her.

A warm smile crinkled about her gold-brown eyes. "Hello, Paul."

He had named his mother "Nonna" when he had tried to call her "Mamma" when he had been a baby. The name had stuck, and now most everyone called her Nonna, even Randy.

"Are you busy?" she asked before she came into the study.

"Of course!" He grinned. "A preacher has to be busy so his parishioners won't catch him idling! But I'm not *that* busy. Come in and make with the gossip!"

"Chesterton said gossip is a wonderful thing!" she said.

"It could be at that. If we gossiped about the right thing. About the Gospel, for instance."

She entered the study and sat in the chair he indicated. "Where's Randy?"

"Always it's Randy! I never rate any attention these days!"

She smiled at him. "I suppose a mother should pay some attention to her son, even if he is a great overgrown ox!"

"Ha! How can a man compete with a runt like Randy?"

"He's still cute, this Randy. You were cute once, did you know that?"

"I must have been. Look at me now!" He went to her and patted her cheek. "Anyhow, I still have a cute mother."

"But this Randy, he's something special, somehow."

He glowered. "All right. Let's go see the little supplanter!"

She got up and going to him kissed him, her brown-gold look speaking her tenderness. Together they walked toward the manse which was nearby. The yard was close cropped and green in spite of the lack of rain. Roses grew along the walk. The manse had a clean look about it.

On the porch Nonna turned and glanced up at the cross that gleamed in the sun above Christ Church. She said soberly, "It's nice having a son run a church like that!"

18

He frowned. "How often must I tell you that I'm not running the church? There are times when I think it's the other way around — the church is running me!"

"Such talk from the most important minister in Sheola!"

He laughed. "Even if that were true, in a town like that he still wouldn't be too important!"

"You keep trying, preacher. Give it the best you have. You'll make it a fine church. And if you don't quite become immortal, all right. Maybe Randy can take up where you leave off!"

"Sure, oh, sure. Randy. The future bigwig."

Inside the house Ann said, "Randy is having his nap."

"I'll just tiptoe in and have a peek at him," said Nonna, "if it's all right."

"It's all right," Ann replied.

Ann watched Nonna go into the room where Randy was. She turned to Paul. "I hope she doesn't wake him."

"If she does she'll rock him back to sleep. Nobody rocks a kid back to sleep more efficiently than Nonna. I should know."

But a moment later Nonna came out holding Randy by the hand.

"He wasn't sleeping," explained Nonna. "He was under the bed."

"I was looking for something," said Randy.

"I'll rock him," said Nonna.

"Rock him?" cried Paul. "He's big enough to sleep without rocking. Rocking is for babies. Randy's almost a man."

"How old were you when I last rocked you?" demanded Nonna. "You were far bigger than Randy."

Paul flung out his hands in mock despair. "I've got to get back to work on a sermon. You women go ahead and spoil my son!"

He was at the door of the study when he saw his brother driving up. The latter got out of his car. He was almost as tall as Paul, and heavier. His movements were those of a healthy man; he was muscular, darkly tanned, and he had light brown eyes, the color of his mother's. He narrowed his eyes when he concentrated. He wore blue denims and a bright blue sport shirt open at the throat.

"Hi, Matt," said Paul. "Come in."

Just as they were about to enter the study, Randy, still clad in pajamas, rushed out of the house to them.

"I got away!" he exulted.

Matt reached for Randy, scooping him up and holding him high in the air, turning him about, laughing up at him.

"Well, fellow, have you knocked off any Apaches lately?"

"Sure," said Randy. "Lots of 'em."

"Yeah? Really?"

"Sure. I got some racapoons, too."

"Racapoons? What on earth is a racapoon?"

Randy was scornful. "Everybody knows what racapoons is. Don't you know what racapoons is?"

"Why, of course," laughed Matt. "But you know what I wish?"

"What?"

"I wish I had a kid just like you." There was an old grief in Matt's voice.

"Okay!" said Randy.

"Okay, what?"

"Okay, you can have me!"

"Fine!" said Paul. "Just like that, huh?"

"Well," murmured Randy, "maybe not just like that, maybe." He grinned brightly, trying to make up for a loss of words.

"Thanks, just the same, fellow," Matt muttered. "Even if your pop wants to be selfish about you."

He put Randy down and Randy started scampering away, for he saw Nonna approaching. But he stopped after a quick dash of a few yards and returned to Nonna.

Paul and Matt stepped into the study. Matt sank down on a seat, his eyes clinging a moment to a picture on the wall. The picture was of a man with a small mustache and curly hair.

"The elder Jenner was a good-looking guy, huh?" said Matt.

Paul glanced at the portrait of his father. But as usual he did not see the Ellis Jenner in the picture. He saw the one of his childhood, a sensitive man with green-tinged blue eyes, a man with kindness in him. He saw a man with vast dreams in him, but who would never see the dreams come true. For Ellis Jenner did not have either the strength or the initiative to build the empire that haunted him.

Paul clearly remembered having heard two oil men discussing Ellis Jenner once. One of the men had said, "Poor Ellis! He keeps grabbing at the sky and sticking in a mudhole!"

Matt said abruptly, "Paul, I want to talk to you about Cal Young."

Paul frowned deeply, his face tightening. "I was afraid you might!"

"Look, Paul." Matt's face hardened. "You're a minister of the Gospel, a man dedicated to righteousness, a leader in the church. When you came back to this town where we grew up I was glad. I figured you'd be ready to stand up against anything wrong, wherever you saw it. But what happens? You have a top guy in your church that's a rotten crook! And you want to protect the guy! I just don't get it, Paul."

"You keep telling me Cal Young is a crook, Matt. But you never come up with any proof."

"Oh, Paul, for the love of — You know as well as I do Young was the cause of Pop's death!"

"I don't know any such thing. I tell you — "

A quick intake of breath from behind them made the two men wheel toward the door. Ann stood there with a teapot and cups.

Paul went immediately to her. He took the tray.

"Never mind, Ann. Matt didn't really mean — "

"Don't say that!" Matt was on his feet, his eyes narrowing. "I didn't mean it, huh? Listen, Ann. There's a man in the church your husband pastors who killed his father — his

21

father and mine! And Paul still insists on making him a head man in the church!''

Ann's delicate face paled. She moved her head. ''But I don't understand — ''

''Matt's excited, dear.'' They all turned to see Nonna in the door. ''Matt always gets excited when we talk about Cal Young.''

''Sure!'' Matt's voice was sharp with bitterness. ''Everyone in this family, except Ann, knows that Cal Young was Dad's business partner in the oil setup. And because Dad was not the hard-headed businessman that Young was, Young took advantage of him. He took him for everything he had, in fact! The shock was too much for Dad, and it killed him!''

''Paul, you never told me about this!'' Ann's questioning look clung to Paul's.

Paul put his arm about her. ''I'm awfully sorry, Ann. I did't think it was necessary to detail my family troubles to you. But don't be disturbed about it. It's not as Matt makes it out. I'll explain everything to you later.''

''You do that!'' cried Matt. ''Tell her the whole story. Then see if she agrees with you that Cal Young should be strutting around the church as if he owned it!''

''Now, Matt,'' said Nonna, ''you know better than that! Cal Young never struts. He's not the strutting kind. He's always quiet — ''

''Quiet, yeah!'' Matt snapped. ''Like a weasel! Like a chicken-murdering weasel! I'm sure he acted very quietly when he pushed Dad to his grave ahead of his time!''

''Matt — '' said Paul.

''All right!'' Matt's face was cold. ''Maybe the rest of you want to be nice to this pious killer! But I hate him! I'll never stop hating him. And I'll never rest till I see him pay in full for his rotten crime!''

''Get hold of yourself, Matt,'' Paul said. ''This thing is cracking you up!''

''We'll see who cracks!''

Matt lunged to the door and went out.

CHAPTER 3

IN THE EVENING when Nonna had gone to her home and Randy was in bed, Ann said to Paul, "You should have told me more about your family background, darling."

Paul nodded in agreement. "You're right, Ann. But I wanted to spare you, to protect you — " He stopped at the last word when he saw the look that came to Ann's face.

"Protect!" cried Ann. "That's the word my mother has used since I can remember! It's the very word she used when she discovered I wanted to marry you. She has been trying to save me from something all my life!"

You're right, Paul's mind answered her in silence. *You've been overprotected all your life. Now here I am trying to do the same thing to you! But you're so little, so like a flower! How can I help trying to protect you?*

Aloud he said, "There's nothing to worry about, darling. Concerning my family, I mean. My father was a wild-catter — "

"A wild-catter?"

"An oil man, something like a gold prospector in the old days who looked for a strike. He took a lot of chances and most of the time he came up empty-handed, and with empty pockets! Though he always managed somehow to stage a

23

comeback. At that point, at least, he was a pretty tough person. He could take it after he got beat up, and come back for more. He had big dreams, but they were never realized. He never did get to be the oil king he dreamed of being before he lost for the last time.''

"But what did Matt mean when he said that Cal Young killed your father?''

"Matt is all stirred up with the idea that Young tricked Dad out of his money and the shock destroyed Dad. This idea has so obsessed Matt that he's wrecking himself over it. He can't get it out of his head that Cal tricked Dad, although there's not an iota of proof of it. I have perfect confidence in Cal Young. In my book he's a top-flight Christian.''

"Have you ever talked to Young about it?''

His eyes fixed on hers and held. His brow furrowed. "You know something? I never did! I must be stupid!''

"Well, you can still talk to him about it.''

"You're right. I'll do it.'' He took her in his arms, holding her close, aware of how small she was. "Don't be worried about it, honey. Everything will be okay.''

She pressed her face against his shoulder. "All right, darling.''

He sighed, still holding her. "I wish I might have offered you something better than this setup in Sheola—''

Her head came up. "Paul, you must think I'm a big baby, don't you?''

He laughed softly. "You're a baby all right. But you're not very big!'' He swung her up and carried her to the davenport, putting her down gently and sitting beside her, kissing her.

"Mmmmm!'' he said. "You smell nice!''

"Your birthday present, darling, remember?''

She snuggled closer to him. Then she drew back and gazed at him earnestly.

"Paul, whatever happens, always believe that I think you're the most wonderful man I ever met, and that you're the greatest preacher I ever heard!''

He grinned warmly. "That's really sweet. Even if you have to stay in a town like Sheola to hear me preach?"

Her face grew serious. "It isn't that I'm bothered by this town, Paul. Though I admit I haven't got used to it yet. But it's little Randy I keep thinking about."

"Randy?"

"I can't help but wonder if this is the right environment in which to bring up a boy! The town is so full of dirt, so uncultured! The children he will have to associate with!"

He stiffened. "It's an oil town. It's rough. But the people in it are probably little different from people anywhere else. The place is ugly, we must face that, and it's dirty. But somebody has to give the world oil. The guy who glides along in his smooth Cadillac has to have power to run it. Every time he goes for a drive he owes these oil people something!"

She considered this thoughtfully. "Funny how you can make me see things I've never seen before! I must be a snob, don't you think?"

"Maybe. But you'll get over it. Listen, these people here can give us something, if we're prepared to accept what they have to give. They can give us an example of hard work and hardship. They can show how people have to live in the raw. They can make us understand what we owe to life. In the meantime we can give them the things they can't give us — the Gospel of hope, the word of life, the example of kindness and love. As for little Randy, what we are able to put in his spirit is far more important than the town we cause him to live in."

She glanced away from him, then back. "You're so much wiser than I am, Paul. You're strong, too. And you're *good!*"

"When you speak of goodness, darling, I can't keep my eyes off you! There's so much goodness tucked away in you it hurts me a little!"

"How can a minister say things so untrue?"

She put her arms about his neck, drawing down his face to kiss him.

25

Presently Paul rose to his feet. "I have some more work to do in the study. If you get tired waiting up for me go on to bed. I don't know just how late I'll be."

He was back in the study when he heard the car drive up. He knew who it was by the sound of the car. When Nonna came in he waved at a chair. Nonna dropped into it.

"I shouldn't have bothered you, I suppose," she said, "but I keep thinking about things."

"About Matt's blowing up today?"

"Yes, and about the effect on Ann. Was she greatly disturbed over his talk? If it's any of my business, I mean."

"I think she'll be all right. We had a long talk."

Nonna drew a long breath. "Strange, your not telling her all about your family."

"Well, for one thing I just never thought of it. All I could think of was how much I loved her. Then after we got married I simply forgot about Matt's obsession. I figured he'd get over it pretty soon, anyhow. Then, after we came here to pastor Christ Church, Matt didn't say anything about it. I thought he was through with it. Now he takes it up again!"

Nonna said, "I doubt if he'll ever get over it, unless he turns to God."

"I told Ann the most important things, I think. I told her I had the nicest mother in the world!"

"You say the wildest things sometimes."

"Well, I knew she'd find out for herself, anyhow. You can't keep a thing like that hid, you know." His grin made her smile.

After a time Nonna said, "About Matt. He has it bad. I phoned him after I got home this evening. But it was no good. He's set in his way. Even if it is the wrong way."

"Tell me, Nonna, you don't believe that Cal Young tricked Dad out of his money, do you?"

She made a gesture of denial. "No. Of course not."

"I'm really glad to hear you say that."

"I'm not sure just all that happened to your father, Paul. He was rather a strange man in many ways. He never told me

26

too much about his business. Perhaps he was ashamed to let me know about some of it."

"Ashamed?"

"Oh, I don't mean he was ever deliberately dishonest. But he was the sort of man who often ran his affairs far too much like a gambler would."

"Nonna, I don't suppose you ever talked to Cal about this. Or asked him how he wound up with Dad's assets — if he did wind up with them, as Matt insists."

Nonna shook her head quickly. "I've known Cal Young since he was a young man. I've never felt it would be necessary to ask him any such question. I don't think it necessary yet."

He glanced at her sharply. "Funny, I never realized you had known him so long!"

"I knew him before I knew your father."

"Well!"

He rose and went to the study window and looked toward the lights of Sheola. He turned back to his mother. "I'm going to ask Cal about it — about Dad's going broke, I mean."

"If you wish. It might satisfy your mind more about him."

He returned to his seat. "Nonna, what do you think of my wife?"

She started. "What sort of question is that?"

"You mean you don't understand it?"

"I understand it. But I don't understand your asking it. I think Ann is lovely, sweet, and plain wonderful!"

"Thank you, Nonna."

"Paul, I love Ann. I love her very much."

"You've told me that before."

"Of course I have! Shall I say it again?"

"I like to hear you say it." He frowned, paused. Then: "Will she be able to make this change from her former life to this one?"

"If you pray enough for her. And give her a chance."

"Give her a chance?"

"She's been over-guarded all her life. It's almost like a miracle that she's such a sweet, wonderful person — with such a background. But, even at that, she's not immune to being hurt, or even spoiled. And *you* might hurt and spoil her, if you work at it hard enough!"

"I?" Then he shrugged. "I know. She doesn't need over-protection from me. But she's so — well, fragile. So like a flower! I feel the need to look out for her."

"Most women are a bit fragile, Paul. Though some of them are not to be compared with flowers! We're a little fragile, but we're pretty tough, too, when we get put to the test."

"I suppose so."

"About Ann. Just don't baby her too much, and I'm sure she'll come through fine. She's done awfully well so far. But you can't tell how much of her mother's coddling has affected her inner being. If you baby her you may trigger the thing — and she may be disturbed. There's one thing on your side, anyhow."

"Yes?"

"Ann loves you very much."

"And I love her, too, Nonna. With all my heart."

Paul saw the gentleness in her face and said, "You loved Dad, didn't you? I'm glad you loved him, Nonna."

"I never knew quite *why* I loved him. Does anyone ever know quite why?"

"Maybe not, Nonna."

"There were times when my love had nothing to do with logic. Another man was in love with me when I married your father. He was superior to your father in many ways. But I loved Ellis Jenner."

"The other man, what about him?"

"It's a bit late to bring him up now."

"I suppose so. This is quite interesting. You never told me before."

"I never loved the other man. I still don't love him. Even though I'm sure he would still have me!"

"Would *still* have you?"

"I'd never make him happy. I couldn't have then and I can't yet. I admire him greatly. But I don't love him, not the way a man like him deserves to be loved."

"Do I know this man, Nonna?"

"We were talking about him a bit ago."

"Nonna! You don't mean — " He stopped short.

She made an affirmative motion. "Yes, Cal Young!"

CHAPTER 4

PAUL GOT OFF THE ELEVATOR on the third floor of the Thornton Apartments. He pressed the buzzer at apartment 310. After a moment a man in his shirt sleeves stood in the door. He was taller than Paul by an inch and quite thin. He was past fifty, his hair a mixture of white and black. His dark eyes were full of friendliness as he thrust out a hand toward his visitor.

"How are you, Cal?" said Paul.

"Fine, Paul, fine. Come in." And as they stepped into the room Young said, "I never quite get used to calling a minister by his first name."

"Try to get used to it where I'm concerned. I get a little weary of that word, Reverend."

The apartment was spacious and bright. The living room had a fireplace in it with ivy in a copper kettle on either side of it. There were several bookshelves; one side of the room was vertical maple paneling. The other walls were light green, the ceiling cream; and there was a blond maple desk. On the wall was a horse and buggy painted on velvet.

"So glad you could come," said Young. "Sit down, will you? You said it was important when you phoned."

Paul sat down on the davenport. Young took a chair. Paul said, "What I've come to talk about may seem rather odd to you, Cal."

Young raised his eyebrows. Yes?"

"It's about my father, Cal. And about my brother, Matt."

The dark eyes were on him, steady and clear. "Matt has been threatening me again?"

"That's right. He keeps wanting to know why I let you stay in the church!"

"I see."

"So . . . I've come to talk to you. About my father, I mean."

"Well —" Young stirred in his seat. "We can talk. Do you want the whole story, Paul?"

"Yes. But I want you to know this first. I have already told Matt that I have complete faith in you. I don't want to hear this story because I mistrust you —"

"But you'd feel better if you heard it?"

"To be candid, yes. I have often wondered about it."

"Perhaps I should have told you long ago. But since you seemed to accept me, I just didn't go into the thing."

He rose to his feet. "I'll get some coffee."

He went into the kitchen and returned presently with two cups on a tray. Paul took one and Young settled himself with the other.

"Your father was my friend, Paul. He was, in some ways, one of the finest men I ever knew. You couldn't help but like him, at least I couldn't. Even if there were times I wanted to stomp him a little! He was a kind man, kind to even a beat-up dog. I always had the feeling that he was anxious to make a pile of money so he could help unfortunate people. When he had money he was ready to give it to help the needy. He contributed to hospitals and orphanages, supported charities, even helped build churches."

Young took a deep sip of black coffee. "But Ellis Jenner was a true wild-catter. He was a hard plunger. He was the kind of man who didn't seem able to tell when he was on the bottom rung of the ladder or the top. He always seemed to think he was on the top rung!''

Paul moved his head. "I remember him, of course. I know about his kindness and his generosity. But I never knew too much about him apart from that.''

Cal Young continued talking, dredging up the life and the personality of his onetime partner from his memory. Paul sat listening, aware of the gentle quality of Young's voice.

Young and Jenner formed a partnership, and because Jenner had more practical experience with oil than Young, he was allowed to make the most important deals. Young had the money, or most of it, but Jenner was allowed to use the money as he saw fit.

It was in the new oil field at Blackville that Jenner made his wildest plunge. Blackville promised wealth beyond any wild-catter's mightiest dreams. But it turned out to be a heart-cracking deceiver. Jenner, knowing his financial condition, still clung to his hopes; and he borrowed heavily on the still solid name of Young and Jenner. He had faith in Blackville. It was one of those awful hunches that a wild-catter might get. Jenner sank everything in the new field. And there was a black day when the partners realized they were broke and heavily in debt.

"Your father had a bad heart," said Young, "though he always pretended he was in top condition. He was like that. He worried more than he ever let on.''

"With your financial ruin, what happened?" asked Paul.

"Well, with our money gone, and our creditors breathing down our necks, we were in a tough spot. But your father figured to make a comeback, even in his bad state of health. He was sure he would yet hit the jackpot, somehow, and satisfy his creditors, and everyone, including Ellis Jenner!

"But he was destined to go down without seeing any of his old dreams materialize. His heart gave out for keeps one day. I have often wondered if he might not have made his comeback in spite of everything if his health had held out. He was quite a fellow, your father.''

"But he died broke and in debt?"

"He wanted to keep his real financial condition from your mother. I was with him when he was dying, and he was awfully sorry for all his boners. He was a pretty sad man at the end, Paul — but you can know this: He was never consciously dishonest. He was just reckless, a real wildcatter. Many a man like him has made millions. But he didn't reach his goal. He never learned how to make money work for him; he made it work against him, really."

"When he died, what about his debts?"

"He signed everything in the partnership over to me just before his death. Which was, of course, like giving a man a deed to a dead cow lying on the town square! I was sole owner of the Young-Jenner Oil Company — and stuck with all its debts!"

"That made it tough on you."

Cal jerked his head. "Tough is an easy word for it. But I was fortunate to have some property in Kansas City which a glass factory wanted, so I sold for a good price. My creditors gave me breathing space, for they had confidence in me. I got going again, but it was a nerve-wracking experience. I finally got even; but it took me years."

Paul said, "Then Matt has everything backward. Instead of your crooking our father you protected him from going to his grave forever in debt."

"I did what I was supposed to do, Paul." Young ran his hand through his gray-black hair. "And I did the best I could with what I had to work with."

"Why didn't you tell Matt all this, Cal?"

The older man grimaced and rubbed his jaw. "I tried to tell him. He wouldn't listen to a word of it. Besides I found out he packs a solid wallop!"

Paul stared. "You mean he *hit* you?"

"Uh-huh. Maybe I shouldn't tell you this."

"He never told me this."

"I suppose not."

Paul said soberly, "Matt's in a terrible condition, Cal."

Young went back into the kitchen for more coffee. Paul

watched the dark liquid stream from the pot into the cups.

"I got enough capital together to take a crack at the new Chelsea field," said Young. "You've probably heard about Chelsea. It was a real jackpot, for me at least. There's no doubt Matt thinks I used his father's money to hit it rich!"

Paul sipped his coffee, set the cup down slowly. "But how on earth can we make Matt see how wrong he is?"

"I don't know, Paul. I just don't know."

Paul came to his feet. "Thanks so much, Cal, for the story. It hasn't helped my faith in you; but it's made me realize you're a far bigger man than I even knew."

"I didn't tell the story for that purpose."

"I understand. Thanks for what you did for Ellis Jenner, even if you had to do it so late."

"My regret is that I couldn't do something for him while he was on his feet."

Paul moved into the apartment corridor and Young followed him.

Paul said, "I'll see you in church Sunday."

"Right." The tall man smiled suddenly. "You know something? I used to be anything but a church man or a Christian."

"I've wondered about that."

"I used to think religion was for addle-headed characters. But when I was wallowing around that bottom rung on the ladder, with everything in the world seemingly stacked against me, I looked up from the bottom and saw the light above."

"I'm glad."

"I got hold of a Gideon Bible in a crummy little hotel where I was staying. I sat down with the smell of that joint in my nose and started reading the Book. I read the book of Romans and it didn't add up for me. However, one little thing in it got stuck in my craw. That part about the Gospel being the power of God to salvation to everyone who believed. Then I got over in Timothy and found this: *I know whom I have believed, and am persuaded that he is able to keep that which I have committed unto him against that day.'*

"And all at once I knew I needed Someone to commit my life to! And I wanted to *know* God, as the Apostle had. I knelt down in that little hole of a room and when I got up on my feet I knew I had found Christ!

"I'll always believe that that was why I was able to ride out the storm and crawl up out of the fix I was in. I got help from heaven."

Paul acquiesced with his head. "Yes. I'm sure you did." He caught the older man's hand, gripping it hard.

CHAPTER 5

MATT JENNER WAS IN THE LIVING ROOM of his home going restlessly through the evening paper. He scanned the headlines, flipped over the pages, took a running look at the sport section. He started to read an editorial, but grunted, and put the paper on the floor.

Through the doorway beyond the living room he could see his wife, Phyllis, getting the evening meal. The light made her gold-colored hair even more golden. She was trim and neat and tall.

But gazing at her Matt thought of Randy Jenner.

What a kid that is! he thought.

He crossed the room and snapped on the television set. Hoofs thundered as men galloped over a hill after some other galloping men. He snapped off the set.

Kid stuff, his mind said. *Kids go for it. We'll never have a kid!*

His memory brought back the pitying face of the doctor who had told Phyllis and him that they would never have a child. There was an urge in him to get up and rend something with his naked hands, to kick something to pieces.

Phyllis called to him from the dining room, and he went

in and sat down at the table. For an instant he envisioned Randy sitting across from him, saying, "Let's eat, Dad!" He shut his eyes. Phyllis bowed her head above her plate and he waited in silence while she asked a blessing on the food. Then he began to eat, but the food did not taste good to him. He knew Phyllis was not to blame, for she was a fine cook.

Phyllis said, "I forgot to tell you. Paul phoned a while ago. He's coming over tonight to see you."

"Did he say why?"

"Does he need a special reason to visit his brother?"

He scowled and jabbed at a piece of roast beef. "Paul and I just don't agree on some things."

Phyllis put down her fork and her blue-gray eyes studied her husband across the table.

"Paul is a wonderful man, Matt. You must know that."

He chewed thoughtfully, not looking at her.

"Funny," he mused.

"What's funny, Matt?"

"What the years do to you! Paul and I used to be very close. We were inseparable. Each seemed to be lost when the other wasn't with him. Now we scarcely ever see each other, and we live in the same town!"

"All right. But you know whose fault that is, don't you?"

"It isn't my fault. It's nobody's fault, I guess. It's just the way the ball bounces, as the guy said. It's life. We went different ways. I followed the oil game, like our dad. Paul took up preaching. So we're just in two different worlds, that's all. We haven't too much to talk about."

"There are some things in the world more important than oil!"

He managed a faint smile of irony. "Sure, sure. But what are they?"

"There's something more important than making money, building a fortune in oil. A man like you never has time to live! You don't even attend church."

"Tell me, Phyllis, do you really like to go to church?"

"Yes, I do. I even wish I were a Christian!"

He set his eyes on her; she was not far from tears.

"Well, for heaven's sake! Go to church! Be a Christian! Is anyone stopping you?"

"Don't you think a woman likes to have her husband go to church with her?"

"I'll be a monkey's butler! What brought all this on?"

"Matt, I just can't understand you at all. Here your brother is a minister of the Gospel. And you never even go hear the man preach. I'd think you'd be so proud of him as a leader in the church that you'd — oh, I just don't understand you, Matt!"

"Look, honey. I just don't *want* to hear the man preach! I just don't believe what the man preaches! I don't believe in the church; they're a batch of phonies in my book. If you don't think so, just take a look at some of the members in Paul's outfit! Like Cal Young, for instance."

"Oh, here we go again! Cal Young — Cal Young! Can't we ever forget Cal Young?"

He struck the table and the coffee cups jumped. "Don't tell me what or who to forget!"

Phyllis drew back from his anger. "All right, Matt. I'm sorry. I didn't mean to upset you."

He rose and left the table, strode into the living room.

"Please, Matt — " she called after him.

He did not answer. She heard the paper rustle, then heard him crush it in his hands. She gave a long sigh. She got up and began gathering up the soiled dishes.

He has built a wall between us, she thought. *He's built a wall between himself and everyone else! I don't know what to do, I just don't know.*

The kitchen doorbell buzzed and she went to answer it.

"Hello, Paul. Please come in. Matt's in the living room."

He examined her face and said, "Are you all right, Phyllis?"

She tried to efface the disturbed expression with a smile. "I'm all right, Paul. I'm fine."

He followed her into the living room, seeing the hooked

rug with the roses in the center and the tufted loveseats.

Matt grunted, "Hi, Paul."

Phyllis returned to her work in the kitchen. Paul sank on the davenport, hesitated, then said, "I want to talk to you again, Matt. About Cal Young."

Matt's half-smile was cool. "I'll be glad to talk about him — that is if you've decided to line up with me against him!"

Paul's head made a quick denial. "I've come to explain to you how really wrong you are about the man."

"Again? You've come to tell me *again?* You never do give up, do you?"

"I want you to listen. I've just come from a long talk with Young. He told me the whole story about Dad."

Matt nodded grimly. "Oh, sure. I can hear the big slob telling you! The same old cock-and-bull story! How he's as innocent as a fresh-born baby! Listen, he gave me the same old gush!"

"And your answer was to hit him!"

Matt stiffened in his seat. "All right. So I socked the slob! I should have socked him harder. Maybe I should have finished him off for keeps!" There was a glitter in Matt's eyes.

"I've just got to make you hear me, Matt — "

"Oh, no! You hear *me!* I'm having no part whatever in toadying to Cal Young! I hate his very insides! And don't come up with any pig-wash about his innocence. He's about as innocent as Moscow!"

Paul's face reflected his agitation. "You're getting in a terrible condition, Matt! You've let this wild idea of yours make you as wrong as a kitten in a dogfight. It's driving you balmy!"

Matt's face tightened, grew darker. "All right — *Reverend!* You just go right ahead and practice your turn-the-other-cheek gospel! But don't stick your gospel under my nose! You're that traitor, that Judas, you preach about! You've walked out on me and left me to settle with my father's killer alone! And you make me real sick!"

39

"How many times do I have to tell you that Cal Young was Dad's best friend?"

"No matter how many times you tell me I won't believe it. Go right on — consort with that stinking crook, make him the assistant pastor of your church if you feel like it. But get this straight. I'm going to cut the ground right out from under the big slob's feet. Do you hear me?"

"Please, Matt!" Phyllis had come in from the kitchen. "Must you act like a madman?"

Matt whirled on her. "You keep out of this!"

Paul took a long breath. "I'm sorry for you, Matt. I'm awfully sorry."

"You'd better be sorry for that precious crook you're protecting!"

Paul's shoulders drooped and he went wordlessly back to the kitchen door. Phyllis followed him out to the porch. "Heaven help him, Paul! What will we do with him?"

He touched her arm. "We must turn him over to God, Phyllis. That's all I know to do."

He went to his car and got in. He said aloud, "Who would have dreamed Matt Jenner would ever be like this?"

As he drove home his mind refused to remain in the present. It fled back to other days, back to the warm comradeship he had once shared with his brother.

He and Matt sat by a yellow campfire along Cherokee Creek, the smoke stinging their nostrils. The fire leaped and crackled, then made its whispering sound. Off in the blackjacks an owl hooted his tiresome question. Slightly below their fire the creek gleamed. The night was soft and warm around them like a great star-spattered wigwam. They seemed alone in the world, comrades of the empty wild.

Paul broke the quiet. "What are we going to do, Matt, when we grow up?"

Matt grinned at him through the yellow glow. "What are we going to do when *we* grow up? Look, tadpole, you're twelve. Right?"

"Sure. Why?"

"Me, I'm sixteen. I'm almost a man. You can see that, can't you? You're still just a kid."

"Okay, so you're almost a man. Aren't we still pals, even if you're a man?"

Matt laughed softly in the firelight. "Don't be stupid. We'll always be pals."

"Always, Matt?"

"You heard me. Always."

"I'm real glad, Matt."

Matt reached and rumpled Paul's hair. "I'm with you, kid, come what may. If ever they want to mess with you they've got to take on your big brother. Okay?"

"Okay!" Paul felt warmth roll through him. But he said, "But you didn't tell me what you thought we'd be when we grow up."

"What is there to be, kid, but a couple of rich oil men?"

"Dad's an oil man. He's not rich."

"Oh, he has to be rich, a few times! He's had a rough time, that's all. He'll hit it yet, you'll see. He'll be rich yet."

"Are you sure?"

"Of course I'm sure. He'll be rich. I'll be rich, so will you. We'll all be rich. The rich Jenners, people will say."

"I don't want to be rich!"

"You don't — *what?* What did you say, stupid?"

"I just said I don't want to be rich."

"You must be crazy!"

"I just want to help people."

"What do you mean you just want to help people?"

"Well, there are many ways you might help 'em. But the way I'm going to help 'em, I'm going to be a preacher!"

Matt's head wagged with incredulity. "Kid, you're real looney!"

"I'm not looney, Matt. I know what I'm going to be. I'm going to be a minister. Like our pastor, Mr. Smith. I like to hear him preach. I'm going to be like him. I'm going to be like him, and like Nonna, too."

"Nonna's not a preacher, goof!"

"She's almost a preacher. She's the next thing to one! She's a real swell Christian, isn't she?"

"All right, so she's a swell Christian. But you can be a Christian without preaching, for heaven's sake!"

"Are you a Christian, Matt?"

"Am I a Christian? Look, don't I go to Sunday school every Sunday? Don't I stay and hear your Mr. Smith preach?"

"I'm not talking about going to Sunday school, or about going to church, or hearing Mr. Smith preach. I'm talking about are you a Christian, a real sure-enough Christian?"

Matt examined him with a long look. "Sometimes, kid, you make me wonder about you. Do you know what you're talking about, about being a real Christian?"

Paul nodded quickly. "Sure I know! Haven't you been listening when Mr. Smith preached the Gospel? He preaches you can *know* God. You know what I mean — "

"No, I don't know what you mean. I don't think you do, either!"

"Oh, yes I do! The other night I couldn't sleep, thinking about what Mr. Smith had preached. You were snoring away, but I couldn't sleep. I got out of bed and knelt down and started praying. I never felt so sinful in all my life! I knew if God didn't help me I was lost!"

Matt was silent, gazing at him in the yellow light. Paul said, "And God heard me! God heard me, Matt, and I heard from Him, too."

"You — heard — from God?"

"Yes, I did. His Spirit came to me. I knew my sins were gone! I was like a new guy! I felt like — well, like I had been washed real clean — "

"Boy, the things that happen to you!"

"And you know something else, Matt? The next night I was praying and that's when I felt I was going to be a preacher."

Matt got slowly to his feet and began stamping out the campfire. As he put out the last spark and they stood in the starlight, Matt said, "Let's go home, kid. You'd better sleep it off!"

"Some day you'll see me standing in the pulpit, Matt!" said Paul.

"Not me, kid. If you take up that business I won't come to hear you. I'll be too busy in the oil business. Too busy getting rich."

A silence fell, broken by Paul. "Can't we still be pals, Matt — even if I preach and you get rich in oil?"

Matt laughed in the darkness. He put his arm across his brother's shoulders.

"Like I told you, kid, we'll always be pals."

Now, driving home from Matt's place, Paul was nagged sharply by his memory. He had been right in his prediction; he had become a minister. At thirty-two he was now pastor of the very church in which he had heard the Reverend James Smith preach.

He did not drive directly to the manse. He went by Nonna's house. As he entered her small, clean, bright place she studied his face anxiously.

"What is it, Paul?"

"I'm disturbed about Matt, Nonna. What shall I do about him?"

Nonna said, "I feel terrible about this, Paul. Matt is your brother; you were like two eggs in a nest."

"I've just been thinking about our boyhood days. Who could have guessed it would come to this? We had a real fuss a while ago!"

"You mean it, Paul?"

"Yes. We have a big wall between us now."

"We'll have to do a lot of praying, Paul. God can help get you back together again."

"Most of all we must pray for Matt. He needs God terribly, even if he isn't aware that he needs Him."

"I know that."

"He's blind as a bat to his needs. Hate has made him blind."

"Let's have prayer for him right now, Paul."

"All right. And let's pray for Ann, too. Oh, there are so many people to pray for — and so many things to pray about!"

"And we need to pray for each other, dear."

"Will you pray especially for me? I need it, Nonna. I really need it."

CHAPTER 6

WHEN PAUL REACHED THE MANSE Ann was in bed, though still awake.

"I wondered what happened," she said. "It's rather late."

"I went to see Matt."

She sat up in bed. "What happened?"

His face saddened. "We're still at odds, honey. But don't trouble yourself about it."

"Paul, I'm supposed to trouble myself about what concerns you. I'm your wife. Don't keep me out of your life!"

He started slightly. He went to the bed and sat down on the edge of it.

"Have I done that, Ann?"

"In many ways it seems to me you have."

"Please forgive me, will you? I want you inside my life more than I want anyone on earth."

"I love to hear you say that."

"Then I'll keep saying it, darling. I need you in my life."

Ann appeared pensive. "I don't think anyone ever

needed *me!* They've always made me feel I needed them!''

"Well, consider yourself needed henceforth — by Paul Jenner!''

She hugged him tightly. Then she said, "We must pray much for Matt.''

"Yes. That's what Nonna just said. She and I have prayed for him.''

Her face reflected some inner feeling. "I wish — I wish I might have prayed together with you!''

I must remember this! he thought. *I must not leave her out.* . . .

She asked abruptly, "Paul, do you think I'll make Randy as good a mother as Nonna has been for you?''

He caught her to him. "Darling, you'll make the finest mother in the whole world. The finest mother, and the sweetest wife!''

The following afternoon when Paul had returned from his customary two-mile walk he met Ann at the door of the study.

"Have you seen Randy, Paul?'' Ann asked.

"I just got back from a walk.''

"I've lost track of him. I was thinking you were in the study and he was with you.''

"Never mind. I have an idea where he is. I'll fetch him for you.''

He passed through the study and into the auditorium to the door marked, "Secretary." He rapped and Carla Brown said, "Come in.''

Carla was on her knees with her arms about Randy, a light in her hazel eyes. Randy had been listening intently to something she was telling him about a big white cow with a black tail.

Carla rose to her feet, standing tall and slim. She said, "He likes cows.''

"It's his cowboy complex," said Paul.

"You discovered his whereabouts too quickly! We never get to visit each other half enough.''

He studied her, taking in her rich, dark hair, the strength of her clean-cut face.

"You like kids a lot, don't you?"

"Yes, I do." She faced him, her look level, clear. "I like them very much. I'd like to have a dozen of my own."

He recalled how she had told him of her marriage to a man named Frank Brown, and of his death eighteen months after the marriage. There had been no child. He had sensed her loneliness as she had told him the story.

He said to her now, "A girl like you should get married again."

She looked down quickly at Randy as if to cover her embarrassment. She spoke lightly. "Before a girl gets married there must be a man!"

"Well, a girl like you should be able to handle that all right!"

Her look came to him, then, almost as a blow. He saw what was in the look, and she did not erase the message before he had read it; and it left him shaken inside. But he pretended not to have seen the message.

Randy said suddenly, "I really like Carla, don't you, Dad?"

He flushed slightly, but he said sharply, "I've told you, she's Mrs. Brown."

"She's Carla!" said Randy with quiet defiance.

Carla smiled. "Let me be Carla to him, will you?"

"If you like."

"Carla's not black," said Randy.

"Black?" muttered Paul.

Carla said, "He can't understand it. That I'm from Africa, I mean, and I'm not dark. I've explained about my parents being missionaries, but he seems to think anyone from Africa should be dark."

"What's missionaries?" Randy asked.

"They're preachers," explained Paul. "Only they go to Africa and other places, instead of preaching in America."

"I'm going to preach in America," said Randy.

"Oh, you are, huh?"

"What if the Lord wants you to preach in Africa?" smiled Carla.

"Well, then I'll tell the Lord — I'll tell Him somebody ought to preach in America."

"You have a point there, cowhand."

Paul said to Carla, "How old did you say you were when your parents died in Africa?"

"I was about Randy's age. I don't remember much of it, of course. But what I recall makes me sad."

"And you came to America with a returning missionary?"

"Yes. I was taken to my aunt in Oklahoma City. Until I was old enough to be on my own. Then I got married—"

When she paused he said, "I'm so sorry about the tragedy of your husband. I want you to know you've been a great help here, Carla."

"Thank you, Mr. Jenner. I have always loved church work. I'm happy with my work here. And working with you is rather wonderful!"

"I appreciate that, Carla."

He reached for Randy's hand. "We'd better go, fellow. Your mother will think you've gone off to Mars or Jupiter. I'll see you, Carla."

Her smile was steady as she nodded. He led Randy to the study. He stood looking at Ann's smiling face in the picture on the desk. He thought of Carla's face and of her loneliness.

Perhaps I should think about getting another secretary!

But he shrugged, shaking his head. This was foolish. Things weren't that bad. This wasn't the first time a secretary had been attracted to a minister; or to a lawyer or a doctor, for that matter! One had to rise above these things. One had to be bigger than that. Especially in this sort of work.

A car crunched the gravel outside and a moment later Cal Young blocked the doorway. He greeted Paul, stepped in and scooped Randy off the floor.

"How's my little buckaroo?" said Young.

"What's a buckaroo?" Randy asked.

"Don't start answering his questions," laughed Paul, "or he'll have you tied up for a long session. His thirst for knowledge is insatiable."

"What's insachel?" asked Randy.

"You see what I mean," laughed Paul.

"We all ask questions," said Young, "even if we don't always ask them out loud, or ask them of someone else."

"Do you like me?" Randy asked Young.

"Like you? I'm goofy about you!"

"Don't you have a boy?" Randy wanted to know.

Young moved his head. "No, Randy."

"Why don't you have a boy?"

Young glanced at Nonna's picture on the wall. "Well, I never had a wife. I once loved a fine lady. But she married someone else."

"Why didn't you marry the lady?"

"You'd better give up, Cal," laughed Paul. "He has a million of 'em."

Ann appeared in the doorway.

"Hello, Mr. Young." Then to Paul, "So you found him. It's time for a nap, Randy."

"A nap?" cried Randy.

"Now don't ask what is a nap, young man!" warned Paul.

CHAPTER 7

From her Pullman seat Frances March watched a small Oklahoma oil town run past the window, and she frowned upon it darkly.

"What a dirty little place!" she said aloud.

The Pullman porter said, "Did you say something, lady?"

Her cool look arrowed up at him. "Not to you."

"Sorry, ma'am." He turned away and Mrs. March called, "See here, porter. I have seven pieces of luggage aboard this train. You make certain you get them all off when we reach Sheola."

"Yes, Ma'am. I'll get them all off for you."

"How far is it to Sheola?"

"Sheola? Oh, 'bout half an hour, ma'am."

"That's all for now."

The porter nodded and went away. She settled her large-framed body in her seat. Her gray hair was arranged in a neat coiffure. Her light blue eyes almost glittered out on the landscape that rushed past. Diamonds flashed fire from her heavy but carefully manicured fingers. Her mouth made a slight curve the wrong way. She moved her head with discontent as she eyed the world outside her window.

How my baby ever stands this country is beyond my understanding, her mind said.

The train bawled loudly as it came into Sheola. Frances March came down from the steps to the station platform, frowning, her quick eyes examining the town before her. The porter smiled at her and said, "It's all here, ma'am, all seven pieces."

She shrugged at him and handed him a half dollar. He glanced at her diamonds, struggling to maintain his smile, and said, "Thank you, ma'am."

Mrs. March saw Paul and Ann hurrying toward her. She stood where she was, waiting for them. Ann rushed to her, clinging to her, and kissing her. Mrs. March patted Ann's back, her diamonds twinkling. She said, "My baby!"

She looked over Ann's shoulder at Paul and said, "My, this is a filthy town, isn't it?"

"This is an oil town, Mrs. March, and a comparatively clean one, seeing they pump oil almost in the streets," Paul said, losing the smile he had brought for her.

Mrs. March released Ann and waggled her wide shoulders. "The place has a bad smell to it!"

Paul said, "Go ahead to the car. That Plymouth there. I'll manage the luggage."

"You can't carry all of it," said Ann. She reached for a suitcase.

"I'll make two trips," Paul said.

"You'd think there'd be a redcap around," Mrs. March sniffed.

"There is one, usually," replied Paul. "But he's not too dependable. You go along and I'll bring your luggage."

As he brought the bags Paul was aware that their expensive look was rather a contrast to that of his four-year-old car. He filled his empty trunk with luggage and piled some of it in the front seat.

"You and your mother can take the back seat," Paul said. "The luggage and I will ride in front."

En route to the parsonage Ann said to her mother, "It's

wonderful to see you again. I have missed you so much."

"You've missed me? Can you imagine how I've missed you? Dear Ann! It must be very difficult for you in a place like this." Her eyes glittered at the town for a moment.

"It's not as bad as it looks," Paul said from the front seat. "You'll find some wonderful people here."

Mrs. March drew her breath sharply through her nose. "I'd never get used to the place. How do you endure it, Ann?"

Ann said, "I have a husband here."

"Hmmm. How is Randy?" asked Mrs. March.

"Oh, he's more than wonderful. Wait till you see him!" cried Ann.

"The dear, poor little fellow!" sighed Ann's mother.

"What do you mean?"

"Think of a child growing up *here!*"

"One would think this was the Valley of Hinnom!" Paul snapped.

"Could we talk about something besides this town?" demanded Ann.

When Mrs. March entered the spare bedroom in the manse she ran a critical eye about it, her mouth thinning, but she said nothing. Paul put her seven bags in the room.

"I'll leave you two to visit," said Paul, and left.

When he was gone Mrs. March said to Ann, "Where is Randy?"

"Carla has him."

"Carla?"

"Paul's secretary. Oh, here she comes with Randy now."

Carla entered the house. Randy was holding her hand. Ann introduced her mother to Carla, and Mrs. March regarded the secretary with cool eyes. Randy stood away from his grandmother, appraising her in a curious manner.

Mrs. March sat down on the davenport and said, "Come here, little man."

But Randy did not stir. Mrs. March said to Ann, "What's wrong with him?"

"He doesn't know you. You haven't seen him for two years."

"He has changed so much. Are you sure he's getting the proper care?"

"Yes, Mother, of course."

Ann led Randy to his grandmother. Randy allowed her to lift him to her ample lap. But his keen blue eyes examined her closely, and he was unsmiling.

He said abruptly, "You're big!"

Mrs. March flushed. "Well! How observing you are, my little man. Do you know who I am?"

"Sure."

"Well, who *am* I?"

"You're the same as Nonna, only you're not the same!"

"Nonna?"

"Don't you remember?" said Ann. "That's what everyone calls Paul's mother."

"Oh? Yes, I remember, now." Mrs. March's mouth curved downward more than usual. She drew Randy toward her to hug him. Randy pulled back from her, scowling.

"Nonna is nicer than you!" he said.

"Randy!" Ann cried.

"Nonna *is* nicer!" Randy struggled so fiercely his grandmother had to put him down. She sat stiff and motionless, a frown gathering on her face, as Randy walked away. Then she jerked her shoulders.

"How have you been, baby?" she said to Ann.

"Fine."

"You don't look too well. Have you been feeling all right?"

"Why, yes —" Ann hesitated.

"What's troubling you, baby? You can tell Mother, you know."

Ann turned away from her mother a moment, then said, "Oh, it's nothing, really."

"Tell me, baby."

"Mother, it's not what you might think. It's not because

Sheola is an ugly town, or that we live in a place like this manse — I don't mind that, though I do miss Grand Arbor. But I've been bothered about certain other things. . . ."

"What things?"

"Oh, they may not be important. But they still trouble me. For instance, Paul and his brother are having some sort of feud — over a man in the church named Cal Young. This fight has been going on for some time, I suppose. But I only learned of it the other day. Paul didn't tell me about it—"

"So he has deceived you?"

"Oh, no, Mother, not that. He didn't intend to deceive me. He just wanted to spare me —"

"But the fact remains he *did* deceive you! Isn't that so?"

"Please, Mother. Let's not discuss it. Whatever Paul did, he did it honestly, thinking it was best for me."

"Very well. I just wanted to be helpful."

"I know, Mother."

"Come here, baby. Sit down by me." Mrs. March patted a place on the davenport. Ann came and sat down. "Do you remember how you used to sit by me like this, when you were a little girl?"

Ann smiled. "I remember."

Mrs. March put her arm around Ann, squeezing her closely. "Ann, darling, why don't you and Randy come up to Grand Arbor for a few weeks. It would do you so much good. You could see old friends, and rest —"

"Oh, no, Mother. I couldn't possibly."

"But why not?"

"Paul needs us both. We couldn't leave him."

"If he loves you he'd be glad to have you take a rest from — this!" Mrs. March waved her hand widely.

"Don't you dare suggest it to him! He'd probably agree! But he needs us. We're staying, Mother."

"Well — I suppose your mother doesn't need you?"

CHAPTER 8

PAUL PRESSED THE BUZZER ON HIS DESK. Carla came in and took dictation. When that work was finished, Paul said, "Carla, things aren't moving here as they should. I suppose you've noticed that."

"We're not firing any river, that's true," answered Carla. "But I think you are accomplishing more than you know. After all, Sheola won't be an easy town for the Gospel to win."

"No town is easy for the Gospel, I suppose. The Gospel has had a hard road from the very beginning. Still, there have always been some ministers who found ways to make their presentation of the Gospel a success."

"You will make it a success here. I'm certain of that. Your work will show up later. You'll see."

"Thanks. Several ideas have been needling me. Right now I want to effect some setup for an extensive visitation program. We have a few loyal and good members in the church here; somehow we must get them into operation. Most people don't realize it, maybe, but a layman can make a greater impact on people than a minister. Doubtless, a lot of folk more or less think of a minister who calls as a man doing his job, the job he's paid to do. But when a layman calls, that's different. The only church that can truly do its task is one that has a working congregation."

"You're right, of course. To really accomplish our mission every member should be an evangelist."

"It was like that in the primitive church. You can read the record in the book of Acts. It should be so today. Every department of the church should be geared to evangelism, to missions. The Sunday school, the periodicals, the colleges, the pastorates. That's what the church, this church, must be, Carla, a mission station to Sheola."

"Yes. As well as a mission station to the world!"

"Of course. I appreciate your missionary spirit. It's rather a natural thing to you, I imagine. We really need you in this work here, Carla. You understand the need of the church and the community. You also understand my burden."

"I'm more than anxious to help you in any way I can, Mr. Jenner." He saw the sincerity in her eyes.

He said, "We have a tremendous job to do. We must put it above all else, above *everything*. You're with me, aren't you?"

Her face lighted. "All the way, Mr. Jenner. Count on me."

He ran his hand over his hair. "There has to be some way to get the church into greater action. Maybe we could learn something from the communists! We might examine their cell-system, the creating of small, hard, loyal cores that keep hammering away until something gives. Their missionary arm is probably more powerful than their military arm. They have spread like red bacteria all over the world. They're still spreading."

"Isn't that something as Jesus intended His church to operate?"

"I think so. The early church had a loyalty to Christ that made them irresistible. They had an impetus, a dynamic, that set them successfully against kingdoms. We must recapture that faith, that urgency."

"Well, let's go out and convert a communist and let him show us how it's done!"

He grinned, then sobered. "It's not entirely impossible, you know."

"If you have faith as a grain of mustard seed — remember?"

"That's right. We just mustn't leave God out of our program, ever."

Paul and Carla became aware that someone stood in the door and they glanced up to see Frances March. They both came to their feet, and Carla spoke to Mrs. March; then she excused herself and left.

Mrs. March watched her go and said, "You have an attractive secretary, Paul."

"You think so, too?" he said somewhat grumpily.

Mrs. March sat down on a chair and Paul returned to his own seat.

"Paul — " she raised her shoulders and then lowered them. Her eyes were pale and cold. "How have you been getting along with Ann?"

"Getting along?"

"Have you been having any difficulties?"

"Why do you ask this?"

"Well, after all, I am her mother. Haven't I a right to know how my daughter is faring in her marriage?"

"I suppose so. We're getting along fine!"

"As you know, my daughter has always had the best of everything. She has never lacked for a thing in her life. She has had money, comfort and my love."

She paused and he waited. "You have brought her to this — this place — away from all she's known, even away from my care. I keep wondering if she can survive — this!" Her hand gestured in a half-circle.

He stiffened in his seat, his brow wrinkling with irritation. "You've given her everything, Mrs. March. Everything but a chance to live her own life as a normal human being!"

Quick anger leaped into the woman's face. "How do you dare say such a thing to me?"

"I dare because it's the simple truth! And before we go

any further, Mrs. March, let me tell you that you're not exactly the sort of person I like!''

The other's eyes were pale blue ice. ''You don't say? For your information the feeling is perfectly mutual!''

''I'm glad we understand each other!''

''Do you think I could ever forget you stole my daughter from me?''

''Stole? We're *married,* Mrs. March. We're husband and wife. Did you consider Ann your private, personal property?''

''She's my flesh and blood. She's my baby. She's the most important thing in my life. I brought her up, dreaming of seeing her safe —''

''Safe?''

''Yes. Safe in the best environment, surrounded with all the lovely things she ought to have — always near me — ''

''So you could go right on trying to spoil her life?''

Mrs. March pulled herself to her feet. Her voice shook a bit. ''I'd rather spoil her utterly than to see her break her heart as a nameless preacher's wife!''

Paul's face grew dark. ''How long are you intending to stay here, Mrs. March?''

A ghost of a cool smile flittered over her features. ''That depends.''

''On what?''

''On whether I can feel my daughter can endure living here in this place with you!''

''Mrs. March, you listen to me —''

She lifted a large hand haughtily, the diamonds on it gleaming as if in arrogance. ''Don't attempt to rush me away, Paul Jenner! And don't try to frighten me, either, or bluff me! I have all the courage, and all the gall, for that matter, in the world, when I need it!''

''You may need it, Mrs. March. I warn you.''

''Long ago I learned to keep little people in their places! I know what it takes to get along in this world. And I have everything that's needful!''

58

She walked hard-backed to the door and went out. His uneasy look followed her.

She walked to the manse. She found Ann in the living room.

She said, "Ann, have you noticed what an attractive secretary your husband has?"

Ann studied her for a time and replied, "She is, isn't she? She's also a wonderful person."

Mrs. March's face wreathed in a humorless smile. "Have you ever wondered why he had to have such a *feminine* girl for a secretary, and such a young one?"

"Oh, Mother! Don't be ridiculous."

Her mother narrowed her gaze. "Darling, you *must* have heard of the danger of young and lovely secretaries!"

Ann colored with anger.

"Mother, listen to me. I realize you think you're being helpful to me in what you do and say. But please, *please* — don't ever insinuate that Paul can't handle his life around pretty women! You don't know him! And I simply will not hear anything about him of such a matter!"

Mrs. March looked sad. "Very well. Let us forget the matter."

"Very well, let's!"

CHAPTER 9

FRANCES MARCH'S FAILURE TO DISTURB her daughter over Paul's having an attractive secretary irked her considerably. For the next two days she moved about in a saturnine mood, sniffing at the air of Sheola. And finally she went to bed, complaining that she was quite ill.

Ann fretted over her mother's condition. But Paul was troubled over Ann's fretting; for he was certain Mrs. March was playing the grandstand for her daughter's attention.

On the third day Mrs. March was up and about, but still brooding darkly. Paul began to feel he could bear her silence better than her bitter words.

The fourth evening Nonna came for dinner.

She and Mrs. March eyed each other overlong. They were not really well acquainted. Nonna had been ill and unable to attend Paul's wedding; she had seen Mrs. March once when the two mothers happened to visit Paul and Ann at the same time during their pastorate in Rimburg.

Nonna was the first to look away, obviously somewhat bothered by the other woman's scrutiny.

"Oh, yes," said Mrs. March, "you're Nonna!"

"I'm Esther Jenner," Nonna said.

"Esther? I hadn't ever heard your real name."

"Perhaps not. They all call me Nonna."

"Nonna — it's an odd name."

"How do you like Sheola, Mrs. March?"

"Must I answer that?"

"No. Perhaps you'd better not!"

"Dinner is ready," announced Ann.

When they were seated at the table, Mrs. March said, "Think of my daughter cooking a meal! She never had to do anything like that when she was home."

"I enjoy cooking," said Ann. "Paul taught me quite a bit about it."

Mrs. March looked at Nonna, who sat across the table from her. "So your son is a cook!"

"My son is a minister of the Gospel. But he liked to cook when he was a boy, so I let him."

"My cooking is the poorest subject I can think of," said Paul.

Mrs. March seemed unable to keep her eyes off Nonna. Nonna tried to ignore her, but finally Mrs. March said, "I understand your late husband was a big oil man."

"He was an oil man," said Nonna.

"Somehow, I can't think of you as being a native of Oklahoma."

"I came from Philadelphia, or near there. My father was a college professor."

"Oh? And you met an Oklahoma oil man in Philadelphia?"

"I came to Oklahoma to visit a girl I knew in college."

"And you met the oil man in Oklahoma, so you married him and stayed here?"

"That's right. My two sons were born here. My husband died here."

"I suppose you often long to go back to Philadelphia?"

"No. Oklahoma is my home and has been for years."

"How could you possibly call this country home?" Mrs. March wagged her head.

Nonna stirred in her chair. "I'm afraid, Mrs. March,

you don't know this country too well. You haven't been here very long, you know. It's quite a country when you get used to it, and understand it."

"No, I haven't been here long. I could say more about that!"

"Then you don't intend to stay long?"

"I'm afraid not."

Thank heaven for that! Paul said in silence.

Sometime after dinner Nonna was in the living room alone with Ann's mother. Nonna was sandpapered at the other woman's overbearing manner; yet she tried to offer her a friendly face. She found this quite impossible.

"I suppose," said Mrs. March, "that you keep a rather close tab on your son and my daughter!"

Nonna's face crimsoned slightly. "I let Paul and Ann run their own lives as they see fit. I keep my hands off. I would suggest that all mothers-in-law follow my example!"

"Do you think I'm trying to run their lives?"

Nonna sighed audibly. "It's easy to see that you are not making things smoother for them!"

"How dare you suggest such a thing?"

"That wasn't a suggestion. It was a flat statement!"

"Why, I never — !"

"Those two persons need help, not hindrances. Paul has a heavy weight on his shoulders, and on his heart, in his work here. He needs Ann's complete loyalty. Ann loves Paul very much; but Ann's never had to face what she faces here. Her problems are plenty — and if you have come here to add to her problems I advise you to go back to Grand Arbor!"

"Oh, my! I was led to believe that you were such a pious and fine Christian!"

"A Christian is not a doormat! I'm sorry if I have to talk to you like this. But I'm very much interested in the lives and the future of Paul and Ann Jenner. I want them to have a chance at success and happiness. Do you understand that?"

Mrs. March's eyes were light blue frost. "Are you trying to frighten me, Mrs. Jenner?"

"Of course not — "

"I assure you that I am not one to be frightened!"

"Let me assure you I'm not either! And let me warn you I'll never stand dumbly aside and let you wreck the lives of these two! I love them, both of them. And I love the church that Paul represents. I think Ann may be afraid of you. But I'm not! And I'll fight you for their happiness, for their right to live their own lives, to make their own mistakes! I'll fight you as a Christian, but I'll fight you! Don't forget that!"

"Indeed! You make a large sound, Mrs. Jenner! But I think you are a huge bluff! Also I'm certain you are a big hypocrite!"

"I will survive your judgment, but don't fool yourself about my being a bluffer!"

Paul came into the room and stood looking at the two women.

"Nonna — what is it?" he demanded.

Just then Ann appeared. She cried, "Mother! Now what?"

Mrs. March cried, "Am I to be blamed for everything?"

"If you came here to keep us all at swords' points," Ann said, "please stop it!"

Mrs. March stared unbelievingly at her daughter. Her face twisted into an expression of agony.

"Well! This is the last straw!"

"But, mother, darling — !" Ann cried.

"My own daughter! I can't believe it! I might have withstood all the others — but not my baby — !"

Ann moved toward her parent. "Please, Mother! Don't talk like that. I'm not against you. You know better than that."

Mrs. March lifted a hand as if in feeble defense. "Never mind. I'm going home. Tomorrow."

"Now, Mother — "

"Don't attempt to stop me! I am going. I could never bear to feel this awful atmosphere, to feel so unwanted. Can you tell me when the next train leaves for Michigan?"

Paul said, "I'll phone the railway station!"

"Thank you," Mrs. March said in a low bitter voice, assuming humility. She glanced at her daughter as if expecting a further word from her. But Ann said nothing.

Paul dialed a number.

CHAPTER 10

PAUL WAS ON THE ROSTRUM Sunday morning, and the choir was singing Zingarelli's "Go Not Far From Me, O God." Paul gazed down at the congregation, seeing the thinness of it, and he was not at ease. He was aware, too, of the sense of discouragement, the inertia, that lay on the small crowd.

It came to him that some novelist had recently lashed out at the church with the words: "You have crowned Christ with insipidity, you have robed Him in apathy! You have made Him a dull, drab King, who was the most exciting Person the world ever saw!"

It's true, his mind cried. *What have we done to Him?*

He faced the congregation after the anthem. They looked back at him without too much expectancy. They had learned to wear these church faces, to be half-bored with their own religion!

Have faith in God.

That was his text. The words had come from Jesus, and he reflected that they must have made a vast impression on the people when Jesus first uttered them — after He had withered a tree with His order! But the words, coming from Paul, seemed wingless.

When the sermon was finished, moved by an impulse, he said, "I wish to meet the church elders in the parish house directly following the service."

The elders sat in the parish house and faced Paul as he rose before them.

"I am unsatisfied with the way things are going in this church! We all know that the church is not moving out for God as it should. But there are plenty of people in Sheola who could come and fill the church, people who never attend any church. Our pews should be filled every Sunday morning."

A gray-haired man named Bert Jackson said, "Mr. Jenner, this town is the most hopeless one you've ever been in, as far as religion is concerned!"

"No town in hopeless!" said Paul. "Unless the church is hopeless!"

"Then maybe the church is hopeless!" answered Jackson.

Cal Young said, "I agree with our pastor. No town is hopeless. There are many people in Sheola who once attended church faithfully, somewhere. But the oil boom brought them here, and since coming here they've dropped into the swim of things; they've fallen into the habit of staying away from church. It's really our duty to make them see how wrong they are."

"And suppose you tell us how to go about that," said Jackson.

"Well, I haven't any pat answer, of course."

"Nice you admit it," grumbled Jackson.

Paul spoke quickly. "There are many things we can do. One is to organize a strong group for visitation — and actually get down to business. You men realize a pastor can't be expected to bring these people in. The fact is many of them will give a minister the brush-off! They'll think he's doing what he's paid to do, even as they are. This isn't true, of course, but they won't know that. Any of you men could make a far greater impact on unchurched people than I can, I think."

"You tell us what ought to be done, Reverend," said

Fred Mackell, "but you don't tell us how! There aren't many people in this church who would get down to cases and join in a real visitation program."

"A spiritual awakening in any community," Paul replied, "does not begin with the careless, disloyal people, but with the church-minded, the Christians who are alert and loyal to God. Our job is first of all to sell this thing to those in the church who are indifferent. It won't be easy. But if we are stubborn enough, and have faith enough, it can be done. When it is done we will have won the first big battle in the war."

Hank Brownell rose to the occasion. "Tell us what to do, Mr. Jenner. I'm ready to do my part."

"Here, too," said Cal Young.

"All right," said Paul. "We'll begin with this group here. How many of you will work with me — with everything you have? Vote by lifting a hand."

About half of the men raised their hands.

"Very well. You who could not feel you could come in with us may be excused from the program. However, if you change your minds we'll be glad to have you. You who voted with me to see this thing through, meet with me every night this week unless you are definitely hindered by something important. It will take some doing, and some sacrifices, to work this out. I want to talk to you each evening about a practical plan of visitation.

"And look. See if you can conscript one person, each of you, to join us in this crusade. Make this a personal job; each of you has a special influence on some certain person in the church. Sermons won't change their attitudes, but your personal efforts could."

"I'll begin with my wife!" said Hank Brownell.

"A good one to begin with," said Paul. "Begin with the ones nearest you, the ones you know, and work with, or love. Sell them on this business. Act like the guy who sold your wife that carpet sweeper, remember?"

The men grinned. Paul added, "There's something else. The kids. We must get them to Sunday school. There's nothing new in the idea, of course. But this church doesn't have a real Sunday school setup. We don't have a bus, not one. And we need at least one to begin with. And we'll need a lot more later."

"I've been thinking about that," said Young. "I'll buy the first bus, personally!"

"Well, here we go!" said Paul. "All we need now is a bus driver."

"Listen," said Hank, "I was the best bus driver in Texas once!"

"You've got a job! Another thing. The teachers! We just have to get more quality into most of them! If that sounds crude, so be it. I know a man who went to the same school I did. He has majored in this business of instructing teachers how to teach in Sunday school. Reports about him are tops. We can get him for a session. Okay?"

"Okay," said several men.

"This job will be tough, but we can do it. We can make this town church-minded, and Christ-minded. We must organize a committee for a complete check-up of Sheola. We'll make a general survey and find out who is unchurched, and put them on our list. George Calvin, I appoint you as head of this committee. You can choose your own group."

"But Mr. Jenner, I'm not too good at this sort of thing!"

"You're a lot better than you think! I have faith in you!"

"Well — "

"Later, when we get this setup rolling, I will conduct special services for a few weeks to try and deepen our spiritual life in order that we can get others to Christ."

Each evening during the week that followed Paul met with his elders; and he was heartened to see that by Friday there were twice as many as had attended Monday evening; both men and women were in the group now.

He did not expect any sudden outburst of enthusiasm, nor did they have one. But there was interest, he could see that. The idea was taking hold of their minds. Session after session he bored in, trying to instruct and inspire them. Soon he would be putting into operation his instructions.

An ancient line kept running through his mind. *Awake, my soul, and I will wake the dawn!*

With the arrival of the next Sunday Paul noticed Phyllis in the congregation. She wore a harassed expression. And after the service she asked to see him in his study. He agreed.

She said tremulously, "Paul, I'm awfully concerned over Matt!"

"Tell me about it."

"He's getting worse! Won't you try to see him again?"

"I could try. But I don't think it will do any good."

"Do you know what I'm afraid of?"

"What?"

"That he will kill Cal Young!"

Paul frowned. "Oh, I don't think he'd do that!"

"You don't know, Matt. He's brooding most of the time. He's even drinking, now. He never did that before! I can't get him to smile, even!"

"All right, Phyllis. I'll see him again."

Monday evening he went again to Matt's place. Matt met him without a trace of his old grin. And Paul was scarcely in the living room until Matt said, "If you've come to see me again about Young don't say anything, Paul!"

"I must say something, Matt. You have to listen."

"You just hold everything and I'll tell you how the land lies. I've worked like a dog to get where I've got. I've fought my way every stinking inch of the way to gain power. Well, I've gained some! You might be amazed to know just how far I've come! I've worked into a strong setup, a company with power — but don't ask me what company! It's a secret!"

Paul smelled liquor on Matt's breath and said, "You don't mean you've taken to the jug, Matt?"

Matt grinned coldly. "Could be. Just could be — Reverend! Like I was saying before you interrupted me — I learned the ropes the hard way. You can see I'm getting gray hairs far too soon! I've clawed my way up from the bottom since our dad died and left us paupers — because a certain chiseler took him for the works! But I've got my hooks in now — deep!''

"You're still crazy wrong about things!"

"I've got my hooks in, good. I'm on my way, now, and nothing can ever stop me! I'm going to wreck Cal Young, see him crawl at my feet, like a belly-shot dog!''

"Smashing Cal Young! Don't you ever think of anything else?"

"That's all I want to think about!''

"I have news for you, Matt. You hear it. You're not going to ruin Cal Young! You're going to ruin Matt Jenner!''

"He's already ruined, Paul!'' Phyllis cried from the door to the kitchen.

Matt sneered at her. "Is that so? Okay, we'll see. I'm top-dog, do you hear? Top-dog!''

Paul gestured sadly with his head. "My brother! I can't believe it!''

"Get me straight, Paul,'' snapped Matt. "I'm going to stomp Cal Young into the muck. Right down in the filthy, rotten muck! And I'll stomp anyone that gets in my way — anyone who tries to defend the slob!''

"Even me?'' sighed Paul.

"Even you!''

CHAPTER **11**

PAUL HAD EXPERIENCED a certain elation over Ann's standing with him against her mother. He felt grateful for her loyalty when Frances March packed up her seven bags and went back to Grand Arbor.

Paul was uncomfortable over his dislike of Ann's mother, but he was unable to erase his feelings toward her. Too, he had a certain fear of her. He was afraid she might yet create some barricade between him and Ann. He noticed that Ann seemed depressed after her mother returned to Michigan. The impressions that Mrs. March had driven deeply into Ann through the years were not dissipated.

For Ann was not the same as she had been after her mother left. She appeared moody and rather incommunicative; she was like a tender flower, withdrawing from a withering sun. His attempts to cheer her up were in vain, and this caused Paul many uneasy reflections.

Even little Randy seemed to sense his mother's mood. "Mamma don't feel good," he said to Paul one day.

"What makes you say that?" Paul asked.

"She don't laugh enough."

Paul nodding, gripping Randy's thin shoulder hard. "I

71

know, Randy. But don't worry about it, huh? She'll laugh again soon.''

"Oh, I don't worry about it," said Randy. "I don't worry about anything. I believe in God!''

Paul caught him up and hugged him tightly, breathing a silent prayer that his son might always hold to his simple faith in God.

One morning Paul said to Ann, "I've an idea, darling. There's a swell little park over by Kenyan River. A fine place for a picnic. Let's you and I and Randy go for an outing. It will do us all good.''

"Very well," Ann said.

In a clump of cottonwoods that loomed near the river they cooked hamburgers over a metal barbecue pit. They made coffee. They had brought along strawberry pop for Randy. The food was good; the park full of serenity. Below them they could see the river lying lazy in the afternoon sunlight. Bird-song floated down from the cottonwoods.

"It's peaceful out here," Paul murmured.

"Yes," said Ann.

"I like parks," Randy declared, his eyes bright blue. "And rivers are nice, too.''

"Lakes are fine, too!" Ann said abruptly.

Paul sent her a sharp look. "Thinking of Michigan, honey?''

Her eyes were level, honest, as she nodded. "I think of Michigan often!''

Paul's face seamed, and Randy said, "Why don't we go to Michigan?''

Paul's face relaxed and he grinned a promise at Randy. "We will, some day, fellow. Won't we, Ann?''

"I hope so," Ann said quietly.

There's some sort of death in her, his mind said.

He concentrated on her fragile loveliness until she gazed off toward the river.

"Ann, would you like to take Randy and go to Grand Arbor for a while?''

"Sure!" Randy yelled. "Come on, Mamma. Let's go to Grand Arbor for a while!"

Ann's head turned. "No, Paul. My place is with you."

"But I could get along just fine for a week or so. The change might be wonderful for you."

"I couldn't really enjoy it, knowing how hard you would be working in Sheola. No, we'll go together when we go."

"Thank you, darling."

Randy ran off some distance, out of earshot. Paul said, "Ann, what can I do to make you happy?"

She turned away, then wheeled and came to him, putting her face against his chest. She whispered. "Oh, Paul — just bear with me! Believe one thing: I love you very much."

He held her to him, his heart wounded for her. She seemed so thin, like a lily, in his arms. For an instant his anger rose up against the woman who had let her grow up unaware of what life was really like. But he fought off the anger. Her mother was not altogether sound in health; there was a sickness of selfishness in her.

He murmured in Ann's hair, "Darling, I love you, too. We have each other. That's so much more than some people have. We'll carry on, won't we, and lick all our troubles?"

Then she thrust him back and cried, "Paul! I'm so afraid!"

"Afraid? Of what?"

"Maybe it's a premonition. I don't know. But I have a dreadful feeling! Something is going to happen to us! I know it. The other night I had a dream — "

She stopped, shivering a little.

"A dream? Now, darling, look — "

"It wasn't exactly a dream. It was — oh, I don't know what it was! But if we stay in Sheola something terrible is going to happen to us!"

He pulled her to him. "Ann, God takes care of His people in one place as well as another. I'm in Sheola because I am confident God wants me here. I've told you that before. You wouldn't want me to run out on the Lord, would you?"

Her head against his breast nodded her agreement. "I want you to do what God wants you to do."

"We won't always be in an oil town, darling. Some day we'll be in a big city church where everything is nice and clean and you can't smell oil in the streets!"

She raised her face and a small smile passed over it. "I know I'm an awful coward, darling. I'm such a *nothing!*"

"You're such a something that I'll never get over you, honey. Right now you are passing through a narrow channel. But pretty soon you'll be out on the broad seas, sails all trimmed, and the ship dancing down the bright main!"

"My poet!" She sighed. "Will you remember something?"

"If you ask me to."

"No matter how things go with us, nor how much like a child I act, remember I'll never meet another man as fine as you. Not ever on this earth!"

"That won't be hard to remember, baby! I couldn't forget it!" His kiss was tender.

The next moment she was struggling wildly in his arms, her cry ringing.

"Look! Randy! He's too close to that bluff!"

Paul shouted, "Randy! Come back here."

The boy turned, standing near the edge of the bluff that rose over the river. He grinned widely. Then he returned slowly toward them.

Ann's fingers touched her throat. "Oh, I thought for a moment he — " She did not finish the sentence.

Randy came to them with a boy's wandering gait.

He's getting bigger, taller, day by day, Paul thought. *He'll soon be a man! Sometimes I wish he would never grow up, but stay just as he is! Needing me, just as he does now.*

The thought brought a shock of guilt, however. He hadn't meant it, of course. He glanced at Ann. Randy must grow up, become tall and strong, able to take the thrusts of life; able to walk the world with a man's look.

I'll be proud of him when his eyes are level with mine! When, without words, we are proud of each other, and can love each other when we seem indifferent to each other. Ah, that will be a fine day!

He grinned at Ann suddenly. "Think of it, darling. We have a son!"

Ann smiled, nodding. *"What* a son! Sometimes I think I'm far too proud of him!"

CHAPTER 12

CARLA SAT ACROSS THE DESK FROM PAUL. Her face appeared clean-scrubbed; it almost seemed to glow.

"I've been thinking, Carla," he said, "that they have a good-sized jail in this town!"

"Jail?" Carla echoed.

"Uh-huh. A jail."

"Were you thinking of moving into it?"

"In a manner of speaking, yes. Many of the men in this jail are not really confirmed criminals, you know. Quite a few are peace violators, and what have you. They got drunk, they had fights and such things. It could be that some of them even clubbed someone, or knifed someone. They're tough, hard men. But they are often men who are unloved; they need help."

"I suppose that's so."

"Why don't we hold jail services?"

"Well, it sounds like the Christian thing to do, Mr. Jenner. But you're pretty busy, *too* busy, I'd say, as it is. Do you think you should add extra burdens to the ones you already have?"

"I could get the thing started. Then someone else could

take over. I've got this gang here working fairly well now, you know!''

"That you have. It's amazing the way things are going. Your congregation has doubled in the last two months! What amazes me most is the way some of the folk have tackled the visitation program!''

"Haven't they, though!''

"But you put some sweat and blood into it, Mr. Jenner. You inspired us, I guess, till there wasn't anything to do but get busy!''

"Thanks. But back to the jail services. Who could do a better job of handling that than a missionary's daughter?''

"Oh — but really, Mr. Jenner, I've had no experience with that sort of thing!''

"Just be a missionary — in a smaller field, that's all!''

"Really, I don't know — ''

"You mean you won't do it if I ask you to?''

"If you asked me I'd try.''

"I'm asking you!''

She compressed her long lips. "Very well.''

"Another thing. How about raising a fund to buy Bibles to give those men? We ought to see that each inmate gets a copy.''

Her head bobbed in assent. "That seems a fine idea. We might call the fund-raisers the 'Committee for Jail-Bibles.' ''

"Okay. Let's work on that. More and more I am persuaded the church must take the Gospel to the people since there are so many people who will not come to church.''

"I feel you are right, Mr. Jenner.''

He gestured with his hand. "Why don't we drop the 'Mr. Jenner'? Call me Paul. All right?''

"If you wish, and thank you. I want to say I'm glad for the interest you've stirred up in the church. And for the feeling of confidence that has been engendered. The church was in pretty sad condition when I first came here.''

"Thanks. The people have responded to my appeals. No minister on earth can get a job done without the cooperation of the members. In fact the members are the ones who really do the job. Actually, in a great sense, they make a minister a failure or a success.''

"Still it was you who got them to working!"

"They could have refused to work. Some people *do* refuse, you know."

"It would not be easy to refuse your kind of urgency!"

"Hmmm. Let's not get enthusiastic over our small successes. There's a vast work ahead of us yet. The harvest is ripe, the reapers still far too few. And there's still something lacking — ''

"Something . . . lacking — ?"

He nodded, pushing his hand over his hair. "I'm not quite sure what it is. Somehow, the church lacks loyalty, the steady discipline, that would make it a terrific force in the world. We sing 'Onward Christian Soldiers' but our army would horrify a U.S. General!"

"Is there a way we can find a method to achieve this discipline, or whatever it is we need?"

"I've been hammering my mind over it for some time. Maybe some day something will click, something will act as a trigger —''

"I'll pray for that trigger!"

"You do that, Carla."

A few moments later Carla rose to return to her office. At the door she turned. "You can count on me to do anything in my power to make the task easier for you — Paul."

His head nodded. "I know, Carla. And it helps more than you know."

Carla disappeared. Paul continued at his desk, working on a sermon for the following Sunday. All at once he realized the room was growing darker. He glanced at his watch; it was still early. He went to the door and saw the black clouds that scudded angrily about in the heavens. Thunder was a great lion raging suddenly along the horizon.

He saw Ann hurrying from the manse, her white dress blowing in the wind. She reached him and cried, "Tornado warning! It's for this vicinity — it just came over television."

He grabbed her arm and led her into the study.

"Easy, now, honey. Don't get excited."

"Shouldn't we do something?" she cried.

"Tornado warnings are not too strange in these parts. I grew up with the things! The warning doesn't mean the storm will hit the earth at this particular spot. One thing about them, they seldom make too wide a path. Even if the path is a terrible thing!"

But even as he spoke he glanced up at the sky and his heart skipped a beat. He saw the black funnel, just over the skyline, making its crazy pattern as it dipped earthward.

"Run on to the manse, Ann! I'll tell Carla. Head for the basement. Take Randy with you!"

"Hurry, Paul! Will you hurry?"

"Run for it, Ann. I'll be right behind you."

He wheeled and ran to Carla's office. He shouted his warning. The two of them ran swiftly for the manse. Ann had just caught up the sleeping Randy, waking him. Paul grabbed the boy. They scurried for the cellar.

Once downstairs they could not hear the wind well, and all seemed too quiet. Then the rain began roaring at the small window above their heads. Hail rattled on the dingy glass, threatening to shatter it.

"They usually come like this," Paul muttered. "Behind a downpour of rain and hail. It's as if they wanted to screen their attack!"

"What are we doing down here, Dad?" Randy asked.

"There's a big storm out there, Randy," Paul explained. "We're down here for protection."

"Can't it get down here, too?" said Randy.

"I hope not, son. You just stick with us and you'll be all right. Okay?"

"Sure, Dad. Okay."

"It's terrifying, isn't it?" said Ann.

"It really is," agreed Carla.

"Tornados are terrible things," said Paul. "But there's

one good thing about them; they never cover a lot of territory at a time. Thank heaven they don't!''

"But what they do to the territory they do cover!'' Carla shuddered.

"Yes, it's really rough where they hit.''

"How long will we be down here?'' Randy asked.

"Listen!'' Paul said. "The rain is slackening. Hang on now!''

A dreadful silence seemed to fall on the world. Then they heard, afar off, the sound of the twister. But the sound did not grow louder, but smaller.

"Missed us!'' muttered Paul.

A moment later he said, "It's gone. I'll run upstairs and turn on the TV.''

He rushed upstairs and snapped on the television set. A voice was speaking. ". . . twister struck Shadville, a small village a few miles from Sheola, and wrought immense damage. The extent of the damage is not known yet, of course — ''

"Close!'' breathed Paul.

He dashed down to the cellar. "The tornado hit Shadville. They'll be needing help. I've got to go. You stay with Randy, Ann. I'll get back when I can.''

Before Carla or Ann could speak he was running back upstairs. The phone rang as he reached the living room. It was Cal Young.

"Paul, I'll drive by in a few minutes. I want to go to Shadville with you.''

"I'll be waiting on the sidewalk,'' answered Paul.

When Young brought his black Chrysler up in front of the manse there was a man in the car with him.

"This is George Rover, Paul. George, Paul Jenner.'' To Paul Young added, "George was at my apartment when the news of the twister came.''

Paul scrambled in and Young flung the car down the street toward the highway that led toward Shadville.

"Right at our door, huh?'' muttered Young.

"I hope Shadville isn't hit too hard,'' Paul said.

"It's hit hard, all right, according to the report. But with the warning out we can hope most of the people found shelter in time."

"Some of 'em never find shelter," said Rover. "Some don't have sense enough. Some just don't give a hang!"

Paul glanced sharply at the man, observing the cynicism in his tone. He was a big-boned man, with homely features, and a hard set to his jaw. His hair was a mixture of red and gray.

Shadville was, or had been, a place of about four hundred population. The tornado had staggered along a path that took in half the main part of the village, demolishing everything before it. It has also zig-zagged among outlying buildings, leveling them.

Already the highway patrol was on the scene keeping cars out of the tornado pathway. As Paul and the other two men walked toward the nearest debris a young patrolman recognized Paul.

"It's rugged, Reverend," he muttered.

"Were there many casualties, do you know?" asked Paul.

"Well, so far I think they've only found two dead. Just see what that thing did!" He waved his hand toward the half-destroyed town.

"We'll go see if there's anything we can do," Paul said. The patrolman assented with a jerk of his head.

The three men moved on, picking their way over tangled wreckage, past crumpled automobiles and twisted trees. As they came to a huge rubbish pile that had been a house Paul held up his hand and stopped.

"Listen!"

"What is it?" asked Young.

"I heard a groan. There it is again!"

"Somebody's under all that debris!" said George Rover.

The three began dragging at pieces of timber. They pulled away pieces of furniture and other objects until they had cleared a path to stairs that led down into a basement. The stairs were free of wreckage and they went down toward the sound of the groans. They found a gray-haired man pinned under a large beam. Beside him a woman knelt, weeping and praying.

"Dear God! Please help him! Help Henry — !"

Cal Young caught up a six-by-four plank and thrust it under the beam that pressed against the man. He put a block beneath the plank.

"Give me a hand!" he cried.

Paul and Rover moved to assist him. The beam came up. Paul set a keg under it.

"There!" Young said. "You'll be okay now."

The man wagged his head in a negation. "No use," he gasped. "I've had it. I can tell."

"Can you find a doctor, Cal?" Paul said.

"I'll see." Cal Young hurried from the cellar and Paul knelt by the gray-haired man. The woman stood weeping, still praying.

Paul said, "Where are you hurt?"

"Inside!" The words came with agony. "Bad. You can't help me, mister. This is it."

"Don't say that."

"Look . . . prop me up, just a little. . . ."

Paul hesitated, afraid he might do the injured man harm. But the man insisted so he moved him a little, into a reclining position, with his head slightly lifted.

"I wish I could see Reverend Bane," said the injured man.

"He's your minister? I'm a minister."

"You're a minister? Okay, Reverend. I've had it. I can tell." He coughed, and Paul saw the red that drooled from his mouth.

But the man said, "It's all right, preacher. I've been living for this thing. Never thought it'd be a twister — but what does it matter?"

He stopped speaking, moved his head from side to side, agony reflected in his gray face. "One thing, Reverend . . . the Lord is right here with me. . . ."

"Yes," murmured Paul. He put his head down in a silent prayer.

The man coughed again and Paul looked at him. More red dribbled from his lips. The man tried to smile. "They all need . . . preacher some day . . . everybody needs Christ . . . some day. . . ."

He closed his eyes, his breath came raggedly. Still more red spilled from his mouth. His eyes opened slowly, as if with great effort. "It's okay, Reverend. *He that believeth on me —*"

The voice faded out, and Paul took up the words: *"— though he were dead, yet shall he live!"*

The man twitched in one more effort to smile. He sighed, a last great sigh. Then he was still. Paul reached for the man's wrist to feel his pulse.

Cal Young came down the stairs. "I can't find a doctor, Paul."

"He doesn't need one now," Paul answered.

George Rover had stood, wordless, while the man died. He was still gazing down at the dead man with a strange look in his gray eyes.

Paul said to Young. "He was a Christian, Cal."

"He was? That's wonderful!"

George Rover still did not speak.

It was late that night when Paul returned to the manse. He was dirty and tired. There was blood on his shirt sleeve from a nasty scratch he had received while trying to get a small boy out of some debris. The boy had been terribly scared, but scarcely more than bruised.

Ann stared at Paul. "Darling! you're hurt!"

"Scratched, honey. It's nothing. Get some iodine and something for a bandage, will you?"

She hurried after the things requested and came back. "Was it horrible, Paul?"

"It was plenty bad. These twisters are vicious things. One man died while we were trying to get him out."

"Oh, Paul! How dreadful!"

He flinched a bit as she smeared iodine over his wound. "It could have been worse, honey. The fellow was a Christian. He died voicing his faith. It made me realize the importance of our Gospel."

Ann wound a bandage about his arm. "Paul, would you be frightened if you were face to face with death?"

He smiled. "Of course. Everyone is scared of death. It's an old fear."

"But the man you spoke of — was he afraid?"

"I didn't see him when the first shock hit him. He was probably frightened greatly. By the time we reached him he was almost gone. And he was resigned to dying. His faith rose up and comforted him. I think it's that way with most believers when they are going. First they are scared — then comes the voice: "The eternal God is thy refuge, and underneath are the everlasting arms.'"

"You sound so certain, so sure, Paul!"

"I am sure! I have the word of the world's supreme Gentleman that even death shall not destroy those who have faith in Him!"

She was silent a moment, then she spoke. "I wish you would pray for me, Paul, that I may have your kind of confidence in God, and in everything."

He squeezed her to him with his uninjured arm. "I'll pray for you. But I need your prayers, too, you know. Always pray for me, Ann. Will you?"

Her eyes lighted at his request. "Yes, I will. Of course I will. But you don't need prayer as much as I do. You are strong, you're — well, you're such a *real* Christian!

"Darling, if you only knew how feeble I feel at times, how wrong about so many things! If you only knew how I fight with discouragement!"

"Do you mean that? I never dreamed it."

"Honey, nobody takes life in a big easy stride. We all crack at times. We all feel overwhelmed by things. Even Jesus cried from a cross-top, 'Why has thou forsaken me?' It isn't a question of whether we crack sometimes; the question is, can we get our feet back under us, and still carry on?

That's what grace is for, to help us when we are helpless."

"You're a wonderful man, Paul! Teach me to be like you, will you?"

He laughed softly. "You be like Ann Jenner! She's the kind of a girl I like!"

She came to his arms. "My husband! My good, fine husband!"

"God bless you, my darling. God keep you."

She was still for a moment, then: "I've been frightened here this evening, after Carla left. And Randy! He asked a thousand questions. Questions! I couldn't begin to answer them!"

He grinned, stroking her dark hair. "You'll never get all of Randy's questions answered."

CHAPTER 13

SEVERAL DAYS AFTER THE TORNADO had demolished Shadville, Phyllis Jenner came to visit Paul in his study. He saw at once her agitation. Her fingers gripped and loosened on her purse. She seemed about to break into tears.

"Is it Matt again?" he asked.

She said, "He worries me, of course. Terribly. But it's *me* that I want to talk about this time."

"Tell me, Phyllis."

"Paul, I've got to find help. I can't go on fighting this thing by myself!"

"Who can, Phyllis? Nobody can fight the battle of life alone and finally be successful. We all need help — whether we recognize the fact or not."

"But what shall I do, Paul? Matt's attitude is breaking me. I feel more and more my inability to keep my poise, to bear up against — everything. You seem so sure when you preach that there is a way to be victorious in life. Can you help me?"

"I can help you by directing you to the only One who can really help you. If we hadn't needed a lot of help He wouldn't have come to our world. He has helped millions. Why not you?"

"Very well. I know you'll tell me to be a Christian."

"That's basic, Phyllis. I have to begin there. So do you."

"I'm ready. I *want* to be a Christian!"

"You're nearer the Kingdom than you know!" His smile was warm, eager. He reached for a New Testament.

"Listen, then. I'll tell you just what it means to be a Christian."

He would always remember her face as she sat watching him as he told her how God had invaded the world through Christ and identified Himself with man's sins that man might be identified with His righteousness. He put the cross before her, trusting God would reveal it to her as only He could, by the Spirit of truth.

And he would remember, too, the light that broke on her countenance when he had finished. She cried, "Oh, why haven't I seen it before?"

"Most people wonder that after they grasp the meaning of redemption, Phyllis. Men seem unable to understand that Jesus meant what He said when He said that whosoever should confess Him before men should be confessed before the angels of God. It seems too simple. We prefer to follow our own complex way of righteousness — *self*-righteousness, rather. Will you accept Him, Phyllis? Will you confess Him?"

She put her head down and he knew she was in tears. She nodded. "Yes. Yes, I will!"

He saw the fine glow in her eyes as she was leaving. She said, "Please keep praying for me, Paul. I feel I can survive anything now!"

"You can. But expect temptations, look for battles! Don't trust to how you feel, emotionally. Trust to Him who has given you eternal life!"

"All right. And, oh, keep praying for Matt, Paul. He needs God more than any person I know!"

"Belive me, I am praying for him. It would be like touching the near edge of heaven to see him do what you have done today!"

87

When Paul divulged to Ann the step Phyllis had taken Ann murmured, "That's one of the things that keeps you going, isn't it? I mean your seeing the results of your labors — people turning to the Gospel you preach?"

"Yes, Ann. This is the sort of a reward that is better than any earthly medal. To feel you have brought a soul to the Lord is a wonderful thing."

The day following Paul had a phone call from his brother.

"Okay, Paul," Matt gritted over the wire, "Phyllis told me. That she got your religion, I mean."

"She didn't get my religion, Matt. She found Christ."

"Whatever you call it, it doesn't matter a whit to me. Just hang on to what I have to say. You're not a brother of mine any more! Quit messing with my life. Don't touch it again! I'm warning you!"

"Your warning can't stop me from doing what I have to do, Matt."

"You'd better mark my words! Lay off my wife — lay clean off my whole life! I hate Phyllis for joining up with you against me —"

"Phyllis hasn't joined with me against you —"

"And I hate you for causing her to do it!"

Then he cursed, his words brutal and hard. The sound of the receiver crashed in Paul's ear.

Paul sat as if stunned, gripping the phone.

Matt, my own brother! his heart cried. *I can't remember when I first started loving you, it was so long ago! Could anything worse than this happen to me?*

He put his face in his hands, knowing that the tears were close. He prayed wordlessly, his spirit reaching out for sustaining strength.

He heard a step and Nonna was in the study. He raised his grieving face to her.

"Paul! What has happened to you, darling?" Nonna said.

"It's Matt again, Nonna."

He told her what Matt had said.

He saw reflected in her a share of the pain he felt. The tears misted her eyes. "When you were both small boys I never dreamed one would be a minister and the other a church-hater! How can such a thing happen?"

He spread his arms and dropped them, not answering her question.

"I put you both in the same bed at night. I prayed for you at the same time, prayed as much for one as the other. I loved one as much as I loved the other. You played at the same games, went to the same Sunday school. I read to you both from the same Bible. How does it turn out this way?"

Still he was silent and she said, "Forgive me. I stand here blabbering."

"Go ahead, Nonna. Blabber. Maybe it will help!"

"We'll weather it, Paul. We still have our faith. We're God's people! Right?"

A thin smile stirred his features. "Right, Nonna."

Nonna left him and a few minutes later Cal Young appeared. With him was George Rover, the man who had accompanied them to Shadville after the tornado had struck there.

"Well, Paul," Young said enthusiastically. "I want you to shake hands with a brand new Christian!"

Paul saw the expression on Rover's face. He said, "You mean —?"

"Uh-huh. George came by to see me a while ago, and to tell me he's been troubled in his heart. We talked it over, and had a long prayer. He's a Christian now! I've been praying for him for over a year."

Paul thrust his hand toward Rover. "This is a fine thing, George."

Rover gripped his hand eagerly. "Reverend, maybe I ought to tell you about it. Believe me, I was plenty far from being a Christian all my life, as far back as I can remember. But it was that tornado!"

"Tornado?" Paul said.

"Well, really it was that man who was pinned down in

that basement. The man who died, remember? I stood there and heard what he said. And it got to me, Reverend. I just never saw a Christian leaving this world before! I hadn't realized what sort of inner something they might be carrying around with 'em! It hit me I could never have managed my dying like that! Oh, I might have *bluffed!* When a man bluffs all his life he can do a pretty good job of it when he's dying, sometimes. But that man *wasn't* bluffing! He had something real. I could feel it!''

Paul agreed with a motion of his head. ''I felt it, too.''

''I got to thinking about that man, and I started remembering the times Cal, here, had told me what it meant to be a Christian. I tried to by-pass such thinking but I couldn't. It's not easy, you understand, to toss over a rebellion you've carried inside you for years. But I finally knew I had to find an answer to the disturbance going on in me. I began to pray for the first time in my life. Then I had an urge to go see Cal. He's told you what happened.''

''I am happier for you than I can say,'' said Paul.

George Rover looked from one man to the other. ''Maybe I ought to tell you something else, men. I've been a communist for years!''

''A communist?'' Paul said. ''Really?''

''Uh-huh. I've put in some pretty hefty licks for the party among the oil workers here in Sheola. I'm a driller, and I know quite a gang of the guys around here. I can see now I've been an idiot! In fact I've been a fool for a long, long time. But I feel God has forgiven me.''

''This is something,'' said Young. ''I've known you for quite a time, George, and I never dreamed of you being a commie.''

''I've got a lot to make up for, fellows,'' Rover said thoughtfully. ''What I've done, really, is to change religions! Communism is a religion, too, you know. It's a religion with two arms, the missionary and the military. The missionary arm is really the most effective, if you ask me. That's the wing I've been in. I want to be in that wing in the church.''

"Consider yourself in, friend," Paul said. "We need a whole army of men like you."

Rover took a long breath. "You men are in a great business, you know it?"

"We're all three in a great business, George — now," replied Young.

"Check!" Rover grinned brightly.

CHAPTER **14**

THE WEEKS MARCHED BY under a brassy heaven. The heat of July was hammering hard upon the face of Oklahoma. The rain seemed to have stopped for good. Even the wind when it blew was hot, and it stirred the hot dust.

As for Paul he felt not only the oppressive heat; he felt the weight of his burdens and labors in Sheola. Organizing the visitation setup had turned out to be rather a strenuous task. He had given his course on visitation evangelism and had got the volunteers started. He emphasized the fact that visiting people was not enough; it was not enough even to get them to the church; they must be brought, somehow, to face themselves, and to face Christ. He felt it necessary to accompany the different units to help them get the feel of the work.

Keeping them at the task proved difficult. There were always those who found excuses to drop out. But he hammered at those who were in earnest, giving them the urgency to go on, even when his own weariness might have made him indifferent.

The jail services met with considerable success. Many of the jail inmates seemed quite eager to accept the Bibles which the church supplied; even to read them, some for the first time in their lives. They accepted the jail services with surprising respect. Several of them confessed Christ in the services.

One of the elders of Christ Church, Manson Jones, who had refused to enter into Paul's strenuous program, said to Paul, "Those jail services. Do you expect to help that batch of riff-raff?"

"Some of them are getting help," Paul returned. "Some of them are being saved."

"Saved? Mr. Jenner, do you really believe you are doing anything permanent for those people? Do you think they will hold out?"

Paul's eyes darkened. "Frankly, Mr. Jones, I get quite sick of people who are forever challenging some minister or evangelist with the question, 'Is your work permanent?' Who can say whether *their* work is permanent? Is *your* work permanent, Mr. Jones? The people *you're* getting saved, will they hold out?"

Jones was immediately flabbergasted; his work among the unsaved had been outstanding for its absence. In fact, Mr. Jones had never been known to state that he was saved himself.

"Of course," he said, "if you're going to get nasty about it — "

"We are not commissioned to guarantee whether people who claim to accept our Gospel remain faithful," Paul said. "We are proclaimers of a faith, not a bond company! Some seed falls on good soil, some on bad. That which falls on the good soil will bring forth fruit. You can't tell whether a man really surrenders to Christ when he says he does; but time will tell. Every jailbird who actually puts his case in Christ's hands will become a changed person."

"Seems you'd have plenty of work to do in your church without going off after criminals!" Jones snorted and walked away.

One thing that heartened Paul in the jail phase of his program was the attitude of the chief of police, a rangy, usually taciturn fellow, with a permanently furrowed forehead, named Claver Brackett. The chief took a fancy to Paul and encouraged him in his work.

"I'm only a lawman, Reverend," he said once, "but I'm one lawman that knows you can't enforce order with only guns and bars. If they repealed the law of larceny tomorrow for one day, and you could steal all day long without getting arrested, there'd be a lot of people who wouldn't steal a single thing! The law can't make a man do right. It can only operate *after* a man does wrong! There's no law to keep me from shooting the first guy I see. They can hang me, yes, but the guy would still be dead! A decent, law-abiding citizen has got to have want-to inside him! I think maybe, Reverend, you and your people can give these jailbirds a little want-to. Some of 'em, at least."

It was a vast satisfaction to Paul to see that his congregation was much greater in size than it had been a few months previous. The church was beginning to make itself felt in this noisy, soiled town. However, Paul never let his gratification over victory blind him to the knowledge that the road ahead was still long and the burden heavy.

Phyllis had clung to her new-found faith and had become a dependable person in the church work, despite her husband's combative attitude. As for Matt's disposition, it still wounded Paul deeply. But he had come to the point where he simply turned Matt over to God's mercy, while praying for him daily.

More and more Paul found much of his time taken up with counseling. George Rover brought his wife to him; and she was full of questions, having been deprived of a Christian background throughout her life. Paul was patient with her queries, with the result that she became a Christian also and united with Christ Church.

The jail services resulted in sending a man to him, one newly released from imprisonment. He was a man who would have been young if dissipation had not made him far older than his years. He was a drunk, if not a confirmed alcoholic.

"Been in jail more times than I can count, Rev'ren'," the man said.

"Do you want to change your life, or just stay out of jail?" demanded Paul.

The man eyed him without a trace of defiance. "I'm sick of myself, Rev'ren'. Sick of my life. Sick clean through. I'd give anything on earth to find a better way. You got anything to offer? I'm ready to listen."

"I haven't much to offer," Paul replied, "but God has!"

The next hour was graven in his memory. He had a chance to feel the power of the Gospel that made the primitive church thrill with excitement. The derelict heard him through, attentive, even reverent in his attitude. He joined in the prayed that Paul prayed, humbly asking God to strike off the old chains and give him a chance to walk the earth again as a man.

Before he left Paul he held out his hand, his eyes wet with tears.

"Rev'ren', I believe I've found a place to stand. I never had it before. Only time will tell, I guess, but I'm going to try to be a good man."

Paul shook his head. "No, never 'try.' God doesn't command us to try, but to be, to go, to do! Listen, Mr. — "

"Gregory. Pat Gregory."

"Listen, Pat. What you propose to do right now is impossible! You can't do it. Go out and live a decent, sober life, I mean!"

"Impossible — ?"

"Yes, impossible. But there are a lot of impossibles in the orders of Christ! But just remember what He said. *The things that are impossible with men, are possible with God!'*"

"Maybe you can clear that up a little, Rev'ren'."

"One time Jesus was talking about a camel going through the eye of a needle. That's when He made the statement I've just given you. The camel couldn't get through that needle's eye, not by any power of man. But God could get him through!

"Your case is like that of the man with a withered arm. He came to Jesus for help and Jesus made the incredible command: *'Stretch it forth!'* Now, that's the one thing this fellow couldn't do! The arm wouldn't work. That's *why* he had come to Jesus. Jesus' command might have sounded like mockery! The fellow couldn't wiggle the arm, but he was told to stretch it forth! He couldn't — *but he did!*"

"He did?"

"Yes. Looking steadily on this Man from Nazareth he worked it. Faith put life in the arm and it came up. That's what you have to do — keep looking steadily on Him. And you can do it, too! Just don't leave Him out! You can walk out into the world that broke you to pieces and stay whole!"

The derelict put his head down in thought, then lifted it. "You sure don't need a pulpit to preach a good sermon, Rev'ren'!"

"Thanks. But you keep your eye on Christ!"

"Okay, Rev'ren'. And I'm coming to hear you preach. Every Sunday, so help me. You don't believe me, though, do you?"

Paul's eyes narrowed. "All right. I believe you!"

Somewhere in his mind was the thought that one of Jesus' most amazing characteristics was His faith in people! He had taken common men from provincial ways and trusted the future in their hands. He had looked beyond their battered fishing skiffs, their awkward peasant manners, to see their names written in the sky. This was one thing that Christianity meant at least. You handed a man to Christ and believed he could come through!

Reflecting on that incident, while recalling Manson Jones's skepticism about the riff-raff, Paul would long remember his joy when he saw Pat Gregory sitting near the front of the church the following Sunday morning. He was dressed in a clean suit, and he had on a white shirt and dark tie. He looked younger, even moderately handsome, and with a hope in his eyes.

This is why we must never hold back the Gospel, he thought. *Why we must hammer this truth forever into the mind and heart of the world, day after day, age after age, never giving up. This thing we proclaim is not a mere creed, a theology; it is* LIFE! *Life abundant! Life everlasting!*

Out of his experience with Pat Gregory was born a further thing.

Pat Gregory brought some battered friends to see Paul. Some of them he was able to help. None came through as splendidly as Pat had; and some of them started, but went like seed gobbled up by hungry birds. But slowly Paul saw the Gospel do its mighty work in these drifting, hopeless personalities.

Seeing this he began to sense keenly that there were other areas in human life just as hopeless as could be discovered in these derelicts. There were men who would never be in jail who were yet powerless to redeem their lives. There were men with wretched, destructive habits, inner sicknesses, even physical defections, that needed the power of Christ.

So Paul, thinking hard on this thing, called on Cal Young at his apartment.

"I've got a brainstorm, Cal!" he greeted the oil man.

"Well, let the storm blow!" laughed Cal.

Paul told him of his experience with the derelicts.

Then he added, "The other day I was reading in the Journal of the Medical Association that a man dropped from a heart attack and a doctor cut his chest open with a pocket knife and massaged the heart; and the man lived. The article also revealed that doctors, nurses and others stopped their work and stood about praying during the operation. The article came to the conclusion that prayer may have more power in it than people dream."

"I have believed that for along time," Young said soberly.

"Here's my idea. I felt, when I was praying for this beat-up man, Pat Gregory, that a strange force was working on him! It *was* working on him! I saw him Sunday morning, a clean man, a new man. Now, if prayer can do this for him it can help others. In fact, Pat has brought me others that needed help already. There must be a lot of people around who need help for various troubles. They're sinful, sick, hurt, full of grief, lonely.''

"That's so, of course.''

"Let's organize a group. We'll put the names of people who have special need on a list, and put the list before this group. we'll call this group, say, The Pray-Roll Club, or something. Every day each of us will pray definitely for each person whose name is on the roll. We'll list his special need with his name and pray definitely about that, too. I can make out a list right now. I know a great number who should be on it.''

"Sounds first rate to me,'' said Young.

"Very well. You're the chairman of the Pray-Roll Club!''

"I?''

"Who else? You must know some men, as you knew George Rover, who have great need of God, who need to be saved, delivered from habit-chains, to be healed, and so on. We all know such people. We'll make two lists. One for those who *ask* for the Club's prayers, and another for those who haven't yet asked.''

"Well, you know I'm willing to do my best.''

"That's why I came to you first. Counting on you is like counting on my right hand, Cal.''

CHAPTER 15

BIG-BONED GEORGE ROVER SAT across the desk from Paul. Rover's red-gray hair was rumpled. There was an urgency reflected in his quick gray eyes.

"Reverend, do you remember I told you and Young that I used to be a communist?"

"I couldn't very well forget that, George!" Paul answered.

"Like I said I was a working communist before I got converted to Christ. I was pretty busy among the oil workers." A faint grin touched his homely features. "I was a commie missionary! They have a lot of missionaries, you know."

"Yes, I know. They have far too many!"

"You said it, Reverend. What the church should do is convert a lot more commies!"

"With that I agree. And I'm willing!"

"They're working eager-beaver overtime all over the world. Their missionary arm is even more deadly than their military arm. Christians had two thousand years to convert China — and the commies took it in less than half a century! And they did it mostly with their evangelists!"

Paul assented to the truth of this, and Rover said, "It's a tough religion they have, friend!"

"How true," muttered Paul. "And too many Americans keep thinking it's simply an army we're up against, something we can hold in check with nuclear power. We're up against a faith. It's an antichrist faith, but a faith."

"Yeah, and you should see what some of 'em put into their faith! I remember a commie I met up in Canada. He was bumming a man for fifty cents to get a meal. But he took the fifty cents and put it into a fund to help get out a propaganda sheet that the commies were running."

"Sacrifice makes any cause powerful," Paul mused, "even if the cause is dead wrong. The church used to understand that idea of sacrifice, long ago. But I wonder how many, in this country at least, understand it now?"

"The church is in greater danger than it knows, friend. The red hordes are still hammering at the gates of the western world. They're still singing about dominating the whole world one of these days. And who can say they won't dominate it if they can't be stopped. And guns won't be enough to stop 'em, or even the hellbomb. We'll need God to stop 'em!"

Paul said, "There have been times when I've wondered if communism couldn't be a judgment against the western world because we have refused to use the light God has given us."

"Might be, Reverend. But still we got to do all we can against communism, because it's the enemy of God."

"Yes, we have to do that."

"I've got an idea, friend."

"All right."

"I was a cell organizer for the reds. Do you think I could get the church interested in some such setup?"

"You mean organize Christian cells instead of communist?"

"Yeah. It could be done. If we could get the people stirred up enough."

Paul frowned in sudden concentration. "One thing,

George. We could certainly try this thing!"

"It won't be easy. The church doesn't seem to understand, as well as the commies do, that it's supposed to capture the world! But maybe we could make it understand."

"It's worth an effort."

"It's a tight, hard little core of people we have to create. We have to create as many cores as possible. They have to be tough. Or at least they have to *get* tough. They'll have to learn the meaning, these people, of loyalty to the church. They won't get it at first, most of 'em, because they've been slipshod so long. They have stayed away from important meetings just because it rained or snowed! But a few could get the idea and buckle down to business. We'd have to let the ones go who couldn't take the gaff. But we'd keep the door open for 'em if they got iron enough in 'em to try again!"

"You really interest me, George. Keep talking."

"Not much more to say, Reverend. But I'd like to work this thing in the church if we could. I worked plenty hard for the commies. I'd like to do something now for Christ and the church."

Paul said abruptly, "Listen. Sunday morning you be on the rostrum. Instead of preaching when my time comes I'll introduce you! You stand up and tell them what you want to do. We'll see what sort of response we get!"

Rover pursed his lips. "The response might not be too encouraging, Reverend."

"Anyhow, we'll find out. I feel you have something, George. Something that could give the church the impetus it needs to do something for God. Incidentally, my secretary and I once talked about this very thing — getting a communist converted to help us organize the church as the commies organize their work! Maybe the Lord sent you to us!"

"Well, I'm ready to throw all I've got in the job!"

"I'll see you Sunday morning. Be ready to lay your plan before them."

"Okay. We'll take a crack at it, friend."

The congregation was utterly unprepared for what followed the next Sunday morning. The service ran as usual, with the organ prelude, the Gloria Patri, the Apostles' Creed, and the Invocation. Then came a hymn and the Offertory and Doxology. There was a prayer and the reading of Scripture, followed by an anthem. Then Paul faced the people, aware of an excitement inside him.

"I'm not going to preach this morning, friends," he announced, pausing, watching their questioning faces. "You've noticed our visitor on the rostrum. His name is George Rover. He used to be a communist. Now he's a Christian. He has something to say to you."

He turned to Rover and said, "Tell them, George."

The rawboned man rose and stood behind the pulpit. If he was troubled over his first appearance in the sacred place he did not show it. His face was unsmiling, almost grim, his red-gray hair somewhat awry. His sharp gray eyes felt their way over the crowd. The crowd waited, wondering.

"People, I'm not a preacher, so I won't try to talk like one. I don't know whether all the members of the church here believe in conversion or not — but take it from me, the communists do! They're trying to convert the world. And they haven't done too bad a job of it in the last half a century! Ask any of your Christian missionaries in Asia and Africa how the commies have made out. They tell you the commies aren't bad evangelists at all!

"Me, I'm stuck with the idea of conversion for keeps! I was a *working* communist, till I saw a Christian dying one day, and something happened to me. I got converted to that man's Christ."

The crowd sat unstirring, their eyes on the speaker. Rover lifted his tone slightly, but he never did get truly loud. But a strange passion poured out of the man that moved his listeners. He spoke of the fierce energy of communism, generated by hate; of its many-armed enterprises, its willingness to sacrifice for its dark cause. He talked of its tight little units, glued together with a hard loyalty; and of the force these units had in a loosely-knit society of people.

He drove away at the cell idea, demanding attention, startling them by his seemingly angry insistence that men should not be soft and careless in the cause of Christ, but laced with spiritual steel. There was a magnetism about the tall, homely man on the rostrum. Watching him, hearing him, Paul was reminded of rugged prophets in the days of Judah and Israel.

George Rover finished his talk and pinned down the audience with an appeal. How many men and women in the church would be willing to join in a cellular organization to take the Gospel to the unChristian world — especially that world that lay in Sheola? Then he sat down.

Paul rose immediately and said, "This wasn't just a talk. We want action. All of you interested in George Rover's proposition meet with him and me in the parish house directly after this service. You may be late for dinner, but that will be the first sacrifice you'll be called on to make in this work!"

In the parish house there were many more than Paul had expected.

"Some of 'em are curious, friend," Rover whispered to Paul. "They'll thin down fast. You'll see!"

Again Rover faced the smaller crowd. He said, "We'll begin with a single cell. I'll head it myself. Later, if we can, we'll create another cell. First we have to organize and test the initial unit, and find out if we can get a head for a second. Let me start by pinning you down, by asking you how much you mean this thing. Don't respond if you have reservations! We may call you day or night to make a contact, to find out what a man needs most in his life, to run down a clue. It's a tough business."

Rover asked those who would dedicate themselves with utter abandonment to the program to come forward and take a front seat. At first no one stirred. Silence gripped them all. Then Cal Young rose and came forward. Paul did likewise. Afterward came Nonna and Carla and Ann. Paul gazed at Ann, surprised, but warmed in his heart. Three other men also came.

Rover immediately dismissed the rest of the crowd.

When it had gone he said to those remaining, "We are in a conspiracy to make men accept Christ! We will use every legitimate means to cause men to see Him as Saviour. We won't be satisfied with merely praying, or witnessing, or testifying. We will use every available weapon to do our task. We must get out propaganda pieces, plug Christ on radio and TV and newspapers. We must each use whatever we know about men to win them. We will be spies for the Lord!

"We are to find out all we can about our contacts, dig into their lives, see what makes 'em tick! We will never use this evidence to hurt them, you understand, but to save them. Knowing a person helps us know how to approach him with the Gospel. You must report to me in person. The man I appoint as under me, the man under him will report to him! No excuses will be accepted!

"Here is a list of people. Cal Young, you came forward first. Here's your man. You know him; his name is Barry Manners. You know a lot about him, but find out more. Probe his past, run down everything that has a lead; make like a G-man. Check everything out. See where his weak spots are. Get his case history. Does he get along with his wife? If not, why? Does he have any close friends, any real enemies? Does he gamble, drink, smoke, or play golf? Stick on his trail. Use the data to make an opening into his mind. When you make the opening, introduce your Gospel! All right, Cal?

Young gazed at Rover. "Well! I never dreamed a man I helped to Christ would hand me such an assignment so soon!"

"Don't accept the assignment if you don't think you can handle it!"

"I accept the assignment!"

"Then don't come back and tell me you couldn't find out anything about this man, or that you were too busy, comrade — " A tight grin creased Rover's face. "Sorry — it just slipped out. I've used that word quite a while. It's a wonderful word. Too bad the commies got their hands on it.

Guess we'll have to fall back on that old Bible word . . . brother!''

One by one Rover assigned tasks to the members of the small group. The urgency of the man intrigued Paul greatly. He kept thinking that the primitive church must have had some of this drive to get the Gospel out.

He did not assign a task to one of the three men who had come forward with the others, nor did he give one to Ann. He asked them questions, and their answers evidently disqualified them. He said, ''Don't feel hurt if we leave you out for the moment. We'll use you later. Soon as you get the feel of this thing.''

Paul was left out, too. ''You have too many other irons in the fire, Reverend! But I have a special fellow in my mind for you! He's a minister! Pastors a church on the other side of town! His is a gospel that is devoid of saving grace. Soon I'll set you on him!''

Nonna was assigned to the wife of an oil man who had known Ellis Jenner. This was her contact. Carla was sent to a school teacher who taught the sixth grade.

''Remember, friends,'' said Rover, ''when we've done our best we will drop these people from our program — but not till we've really done our best. One thing more. A Christian has the advantage over a communist. The early church proved that. We have the Holy Spirit! We must not leave Him out of our setup. This is our secret weapon. We belong to the biggest, finest labor union in the world. Paul expressed it: ''We are laborers together with God!'''

At the noon meal Ann said to Paul, ''I'm not much of a Christian, am I?''

''What does that mean?''

''You saw how Mr. Rover passed over me when he was making assignments!''

Paul hesitated. ''Darling, he passed over others. Me, for instance!''

''He gave a reason for passing over you.''

''Well, he was — sifting out a few who understood the idea of going all out for the Gospel —''

"That's just it! He saw through me! He knew I wasn't fit to do the work!"

"But, honey — "

"Oh, I'm not pouting about it. I'm aware I'm not all I should be — even to be a minister's wife! I have no delusions about myself. In my heart I've longed to serve God in a great way, but I've never got to it. I've sat here and watched *you* working yourself ragged for the church. I've watched the church grow under your ministry. I've watched Cal Young and Nonna and Carla. But what have I done?"

"You've been a swell mamma!" said Randy, who had been listening to the conversation without seeming to.

Ann put a smile of gratitude on him. Paul said, "You see? What more important job is there than being a swell mamma? I ask you. Besides you've been a sweet, grand wife. And I adore you!"

Ann moved her head, the smile disappearing. "You see how it is? You baby me! You try to make me think I'm all right when I know better! My mother always did that, too!"

Her last words stabbed at Paul, and he sucked in his breath. His face grew serious. "All right, darling. I think we have left you out of the program too much." In him a warmth began to spread. This was as he wanted it, as it should be!

He added, "Next Sunday afternoon you will go with Carla and the others to a jail service!"

"To a — jail — service?"

"Uh-huh. See what you can do for those people. They need help — plenty. You can report to *me* how you come out!" He grinned at her.

She smiled. "Fine! Even if you do sound like a new cell organizer already!"

CHAPTER 16

WHEN ANN RETURNED from her first visit to the jail her face reflected her inner agitation.

"Tell me about it, honey," said Paul.

"Those men!" Her slim hands were caught together as if in an attitude of prayer. "Paul, do you realize that I've never looked at an inmate of jail before in my life?"

"There are thousands of Americans who have never looked inside a jail, Ann. They read of people going to jail, or hear about them. To them such people are scarcely more than ghosts. They are not real flesh and blood individuals, with minds and hearts and human needs."

"I — I can't tell you how they made me feel. I think I feel like weeping!"

"Weeping won't help. The only thing that can help them is a friendly hand. I know they're in sad condition. But I'm positive Jesus wouldn't have shied away from them. They would have been an object of His compassion. He would have offered them forgiveness, as He did the woman taken in adultery."

"I must go back and see them again! At first, when I saw them, I was frightened. They didn't seem like human beings.

Then I saw something in their eyes! They were — they looked so hungry! They were like children that have been crowded away from the dinner table!"

"They are hungry, darling." A joy gripped him inwardly. This would help her to forget the discomforts of living in a raucous oil town!

"I didn't really take part in the jail service," Ann said. "But I want to take part the next time. I believe I can say something to those men, something to make them grasp the fact that there is a better way of life than they know!"

He looked at her, standing before him, small and lovely and earnest; and he felt she should be able to lift any man's soul upward. To him there was an angelic quality about her.

One day a bony woman who was still young but looked quite old visited Paul's study.

"I'm Bonnie James," she said. "Pat Gregory told me about you. He says you helped him get out of the ditch. Maybe you can help me."

"Be seated, please," Paul said. As the woman sat down he took up the phone and called the manse. When Ann answered he said, "Can you come over to the study, honey?"

"Why, yes," Ann said.

"Your wife?" asked Bonnie. "Do you have to have her?"

"It's all right, Bonnie. You can say anything to both of us you wanted to say to me alone."

"She's a woman —"

"She's a woman, but she's your friend, Bonnie, I assure you."

When Ann came into the study she hesitated at the sight of the thin and soiled Bonnie. But she took the chair Paul indicated.

"This is Bonnie James, honey. Bonnie, this is my wife, Ann."

Bonnie nodded a little stiffly. Paul said, "Do you want to tell us your difficulties?"

"Well — " Bonnie glanced away from him to look at Ann, then back at him again. "Well, I'm just a no-good, rotten woman. Reverend! Do you know what I mean?"

He nodded. "I know."

"I was young once — oh, I'm still not so old. But what I mean is, I was good-looking. I had something. Now I don't have a thing! I loved a man, a fine young guy. I loved him like — well, like I can't even tell you. He got killed in Korea. Shot on one of them stinking hills. I couldn't get over him. Kept thinking how it was with him out there on that hill, with a bullet through him, maybe twisting and moaning, before he finally died. And me not there to even put my arms around him, and hold him, or anything — "

The woman was crying, the tears sliding down her thin face. Paul waited for her, and she added, "He was such a swell guy, Reverend. You don't know how much I loved him. I couldn't get over it. I saw him every time I saw somebody in a crowd. I wanted to run up and grab somebody and say, 'Hello, Johnny!' I saw him when I went to sleep, and it always woke me up. I just couldn't take it. I started hitting the bottle. I'm no good. I'm a street character, that's what I am!"

She paused, dabbing at her eyes with a dirty handkerchief. "But I don't really want to be a street woman, Reverend!"

Ann said suddenly, "But, Bonnie, you have to have someone bigger than you are to hold on to. Even someone bigger than Johnny. Johnny had to leave you, but you must have Someone who won't ever leave you."

The woman turned reddened eyes toward her. "Yeah! But who, and *what?*"

"You loved Johnny, but Johnny was only human, even as you are. You must have Someone more than human. We all must. We must have God!"

The woman considered Ann for a moment. "Do you have a God, lady?"

Ann shot a look toward Paul, then looked at Bonnie again. "Yes, Bonnie. I have God."

"Can you prove it, lady? How do you know you have God?"

"Well —" said Ann. "God is a Spirit. I have Him in my heart."

Paul said, "She knows the same way I know, Bonnie. It's not easy to explain to one who doesn't have Him, but it's still a fact that we have Him. There's an inner witness, an unmistakable knowledge, within. There's a word in the Bible about it. *'The Spirit also bears witness with our spirit that we are the children of God.'* "

The woman had stopped crying. "If I had God in me, as you do, then my life would be different, wouldn't it?"

"You'd be a new creature," said Paul. "That is the pledge of the Gospel."

"Okay!"

"You'll accept Christ as your Saviour?"

"I want to get off the stinking street! I want to start new. I want to get sober and stay sober. I'll need a lot of fixing for all that. Won't I, Reverend?"

"God can do a lot of fixing, Bonnie."

"Where do we start?" Bonnie looked around at both Paul and Ann.

Ann said, "We should start with prayer. Isn't that where we start, Paul?"

"That's where we start," he answered.

The woman was about to weep again. Hers was the face of one who had tried and tried, again and again, and had lost. Fear was in that face, hopelessness was there. But she slid off her chair and sank to her knees, her head falling on her arms.

"Then pray for me!" she said in muffled tones. "Pray — hard!"

CHAPTER 17

PAUL CAME INTO THE MANSE one day to find Ann hanging up the phone. He looked anxiously at her and asked, "Is something wrong, Ann?"

"It was Mother calling from Grand Arbor."

"Oh? How is she?"

"She's all right. That's the second time she's called this week!"

"Really? I didn't know."

"I forgot to tell you the other time. She keeps at me to come up there for a visit."

"Well, would you like to go?"

"My place is here, Paul."

"Maybe a little vacation from Sheola would be a good thing for you. Don't worry about me. I can manage fine. How about it?"

"No. Not now, anyhow. You're the one who needs a vacation. You work so hard. I'll stay with you. You do need me, don't you?"

He caught her in his arms. "I need you very much. I'll never get to where I won't need you."

Sometime after that Paul noticed a softness in Ann's

face. He kept thinking that he had seen that look on her face before. He thought of asking her about it but decided it might seem like a foolish question. However the reason for her expression became clear one morning at breakfast.

"I saw Doctor Carmel yesterday," Ann said.

"Doctor Carmel?" cried Paul. "Are you ill, darling?"

Her smile was tender and gentle. "Wouldn't it be nice to have a little girl this time?"

He gaped at her. He sprang up from the table and went around to her. "Ann! Do you mean it?"

She nodded happily, catching hold of his hand. "Well, don't you think Randy needs a baby sister?"

He gripped both her shoulders. "Why, you sneaky little scalawag!"

"If it's a girl what will we call her?"

"Oh — what about Jennifer?"

"Oh, Paul! Jennifer Jenner! What kind of name is that?"

Randy, who had been examining them carefully, said, "Who's Jennifer Jenner?"

"Ah, he's getting interested, Ann! Randy, how would you like to have a baby sister?"

Randy took a spoonful of oatmeal and spoke around it. "What for?"

"Just listen to this character!" Paul groaned. "What for? What a big family man he is! Never mind, Ann. We'll ignore him."

"Oh, he really wants a baby sister, Paul." Ann smiled. "He's just acting like a boy. He'll love her."

Paul ran his hand over his hair. "But what if his sister is a brother?"

"Brother?" Randy echoed. "Sure. I wish I had a brother. If I had a brother he could be an Indian!"

"Indian?"

"Sure, and I could be a cowboy!"

"I get it. Cowboys always get the best of the Indians."

"Sure," said Randy.

"A fine family man!" Paul repeated.

Paul was half-way to the study, in his excitement, before he remembered something. He hurried back to the house.

"I forgot, Ann. Cal Young thinks I've been working too hard lately. He wants to take me fishing over on Kenyan River."

"I think Cal's right about your over-working."

"Would you like to come along with us?"

She smiled. "I'm going to stay here, and, well, just dream about some things."

"Oh, sure. Randy, do you want to go fishing?"

"Fishing?" cried Randy.

"See? That gets his interest. Even if a baby sister doesn't. Okay, fellow. You're in the fishing party."

"Oh, boy!" Randy began to go about in circles.

"Hey, watch it, cowhand!" Paul cried. "Get a grip on yourself. We have to wait for Mr. Young."

"Oh, boy!" Randy repeated. "Fishing!"

"Will you get him ready, Ann? I'll get into some clothes myself."

He started upstairs and stopped on the steps. "How about Angela? That's a swell name for a girl, isn't it?"

Her head refused him. "Try again."

Sometime later Paul was in his study arrayed in fishing togs, with his skimpy gear. Randy was dressed as a cowboy, minus guns. He was circling the study, restless as a wind.

"I sure hope nothing happens to Mr. Young's car!" he said anxiously. "I hope his car runs fine."

"Keep your sombrero on. Mr. Young's car will be okay. He'll be here any time now."

Just then he heard Young's car, and the phone rang.

When Young came in Paul said, "I'm sorry, Cal. Just got a call from Mrs. Redfield. John is ill. Dr. Carmel is out there with him now. She thinks he may be dying. I'll have to run out and see him."

Young pursed his lips. Randy cried, "Can't we go fishing? Can't we?"

"Sure we're going, Randy," Young said. "Look,

Paul, you go on out and see Redfield. I'll take Randy and drive to Kenyan River. You know where the road is — remember we took it one day?"

Paul nodded. "It comes to the river by that big bluff."

"Right. We'll be along there somewhere. You'll see my car."

"Sure," Randy agreed, "we'll be there."

"Okay," Paul said. "I'll get out there as soon as I possibly can. Don't catch all the fish."

"We'll save some little ones for you."

Young took the excited Randy in his car and drove off. Paul stepped into Carla's office.

"Carla, I'm running out to see John Redfield. His wife says he's pretty bad. If anybody calls make a memo. From Redfield's place I'm going to Kenyan River to fish."

"Swell. And don't look guilty about it! You really need the rest, you know."

"There's so much to do," he muttered. "I'll be back in the evening. On my desk you'll find a list of the people the Prayer Club is praying for. Can you get those mimeographed today?"

"I'll attend to it. By the way, we've had some good results from this Club's praying."

"Yes. Two alcoholics have been helped out of there rat-race. We have a report that one man was healed of nervous difficulties. Two men came to see me in the last three days who were on the list and they are going to go all out for Christ, they tell me. Things are moving."

"I just had a phone call from a woman who asks to be put on the Club's list. A lady named Agnes Lomarr."

"Good. Put her name on the mimeographed sheet."

He drove out to John Redfield's place, a few miles distant from Sheola. Redfield, before his illness, had been an oil pumper, and he lived in a company house in the field. The dust stood behind Paul's car in a reddish cloud as he drove over the dirt road. It had been dry for a long time. He recalled how the rain had come down torrentially the day the tornado hit Shadville, and he wished they might have a bit of that moisture now. The heat, too, forced itself in upon him as he drove; even the air sweeping in at the windows was like the breath of a mild furnace.

Redfield was a pale, sick man, a man who had been sick overlong. His bloodless lips moved in a whispery greeting to the minister. The doctor drew away to the foot of the bed.

Redfield mouthed in a foggy voice, "Read me — Psalm."

Paul drew out his worn Bible and turned to the Twenty-third Psalm. He did not look at the Book, knowing the poem by memory. Along with the words he spoke there was a reflection in his mind that thousands on thousands of people had heard this psalm read as they lay close to death. It was a great thing that a poem should have lasted so long and given so much strength and comfort to so many souls.

How weak man was! How much he needed help from a source above his own. And how the music that came from a lonely shepherd long ago made the pain of dying easier.

An hour later, as Paul was going to his car, Doctor Carmel called to him; and he waited for the physician to catch up with him.

The doctor said, "He's not long for this world, Mr. Jenner."

"I thought as much."

The physician rubbed his face thoughtfully. "Somehow, at a time like this I find myself rather envying people like you — ministers, I mean. You can take up where we have to leave off and walk away. It must be a satisfying business."

Paul made an assent. "Yes, doctor, it is."

They talked a moment and Paul was starting for his car again when Carmel called, "By the way — congratulations! Your wife wants a girl, she says. I trust she gets her wish."

Paul grinned. "So do I!"

Cal Young's Buick slipped swiftly over the highway. Randy sat on the front seat, restless, but full of happiness.

Now and then he looked up at Young to study the oil man's profile.

Finally Young said, "What is it, Randy?"

"I was just wondering about something," Randy said.

"Yes?"

"I was wondering where she is?"

Young glanced down at him quickly. "She? Who, Randy?"

"You know. The lady you loved and you never did marry her."

"Oh! You still remember that?"

"Sure."

"Well, Randy, she's still somewhere — around."

"Around where, Mr. Young?"

"It doesn't matter, does it, Randy?"

Randy considered this. Then: "Did the lady marry someone else?"

"Yes."

"That's bad. Isn't it?"

"The man she married died."

"He died? She doesn't have a husband now then, does she?"

"No, she hasn't."

"Then why don't you marry her then?" demanded Randy.

Young tried to smile but the smile was rather thin. "Well, to tell the truth, Randy, the lady doesn't love me enough to marry me."

Randy considered this problem for a time, then grinned. "Well, why couldn't you *make* her love you, maybe?"

The Buick left the highway and stirred a billow of dust on a dirt road. Randy was still insisting Young should, somehow, compel the lady he loved to accept him. The road wound for several miles until it came in sight of the river. On a high bluff Young brought the car to a stop.

"Well, here we are, fisherman!" he said. "Think you can catch a big one?"

"Sure," Randy said.

Young began getting his tackle from the trunk of the car. When he glanced up he saw Randy hurrying toward the edge of the bluff.

"Randy! Hey, wait!" Young called.

Randy turned and grinned at him. He slackened his pace but went on. Young moved to catch up with him. He was not far behind him when Randy reached the bluff's edge.

"Randy! Keep away from the edge!"

"Okay," Randy promised.

He kept his promise, stopping where he was and waiting. But he was too close to the bluff's edge. Panic struck at Young.

"Stand still, Randy. Stand real still!"

"I'll stand still," the boy said.

But suddenly Randy seemed to sink into the earth. Through Young's panic-lashed brain burned the realization that a small area of the dry dirt along the bluff had given way, taking Randy with it. Young remembered now far it was down to the river. A long thin cry knifed Young's ears.

"Randy!" he screamed. *"Randy!"*

He flung himself to the edge of the bluff. He saw the dust swirling below, but he could not see Randy. A vast sob tore out of his tortured throat. He sprang for a steep path that wound down to the river's edge. His breath came in choking gasps as he scrambled down the path. At the bottom of the path he began running up-river.

And he saw Randy.

Randy was face down at the foot of the tall bluff. His body was like a broken doll's, inert on the rocks. Young hurled himself forward to the still form, dropping down on his knees, a groan bursting out of him.

He gathered up Randy in his arms, and the small head rolled back limply. The little face was blood-wet and dirty, as was the dark curly hair. The very blue eyes were open, but they were not seeing.

"Dear God!" moaned Young. "Dear God in heaven — help me — help him —"

Frantically he put his ear against the narrow chest,

begging for a sound. Nothing stirred within. Randy Jenner, a moment before a dynamo of human energy, was gone.

Young lowered the body on a sandy flat place between the jagged rocks, fighting against the choking shock. He hovered over the tiny form, as if to protect it from further hurt, sobbing a futile prayer. He lifted his eyes, sweeping the universe; the heavens seemed to mock him.

What will I say to Paul Jenner? And to Ann? Oh, dear God, what will I say to them?

CHAPTER 18

PAUL DROVE FROM THE REDFIELD HOME to the highway that led toward Kenyan River, with the dying, pale man in his mind. The earth had so much suffering! Small wonder the New Testament spoke often of compassion. Paul recalled having once heard a minister in the seminary he attended saying, "Compassion means I hurt because someone else hurts. I am wounded for their wounds."

Paul felt stiffness in his shoulders; his hands were gripping the wheel too hard. He thought, *I must relax. I've been getting too tense lately. I'll have to watch it. A day on the river will do me good. Jesus knew. That's why He told His church to come apart and rest a while.*

He recalled Dr. Carmel's words of congratulation, and his smile lit his features, the smile growing tender. Well, all right! If you couldn't call her Jennifer Jenner, or Angela, how about Barbara Jenner? Not a bad name. Not bad at all.

But what if it wasn't a girl? Okay. Two sons would be all right. How about Paul Jenner the Second? Not Junior, of course. I don't like Junior. But Paul Jenner, the Second. That wouldn't be hard to take, not at all.

This was what Ann needed, too! Now she could concentrate on her joys and not be bothered with her environment. Anyhow, Ann was doing fine at that point. She was beginning to fit into this world, to feel its needs. He heaved a sigh of gratitude.

He left the highway and took the dirt road that led toward the river. He saw the dust cloud approaching, with Cal Young's car in front of the cloud. As Young drew nearer he saw Young in the front seat, alone. Paul snapped his car over to the side and waited. Young's car came up and he saw the oil man's face, and a quick terror lanced at his soul.

He leaped from his car. Young remained behind his wheel as if unable to move.

"Cal! Where's Randy?"

Young turned his stricken gray face upon him, his head jerking, jerking until it motioned toward the back seat.

"Paul — " The words would not come.

Paul lunged forward and tore the door open. He stared at the still body of his son. Wildly he reached in and caught the small body to him, his head wagging a sudden bursting agony, his look unbelieving. But his heart knew! He staggered away from the car, his knees becoming water, and he fell on them in the red dust, clutching his son's unresisting body to his breast.

It can't be so, God! It can't be. I can't bear it!

A shudder vibrated his frame. The shock was too great to allow tears. He put his tormented face toward the sky.

"God! Dear God! What happened?"

Young stumbled from his car and came and knelt down by Paul.

"He fell, Paul! He fell off the bluff. He ran ahead of me — "

Paul twisted his head and stared at Young as if he were an utter stranger.

"He fell?"

Young gulped hard, nodded, his face a mask of pain. "I tried to reach him. God knows I tried to reach him! But the ground gave away —"

"He's *dead!*"

It was a cry with all the grief in the world in it. And quickly another cry followed it.

"Ann! What will we tell Ann?"

He staggered to his feet, holding Randy tightly to his heart. His own heart hammered, but Randy's was still.

"We've got to tell Ann. This will kill her! This will kill her — if we can't help her — !"

Young had gained some composure. "Paul, listen. Can you drive?"

"Drive?"

"I'll go ahead and tell Ann. Can you drive — and bring Randy?"

Paul stared at him as if he did not understand. Then he nodded his head. "I can drive. Go ahead, Cal. I'll bring my — son!"

Young went to his car. It roared away. Paul put Randy down gently on the front seat. He got in behind the wheel. There was a stoniness about his features. He drew Randy's blood-smeared head on his lap. Then all the stone melted in his face and his grief came in hot, terrible tears. He put his face down on the steering wheel, sobbing, with his whole frame shaking.

He did not know how long he sat there. But at last he straightened up, wiping his wet face with a trembling hand. He looked down at Randy again.

He said aloud, "I've got to help Ann, somehow—"

He drove toward the highway, with the landscape blurred in his vision. He knew now there were such sorrows as cannot be told; they must be experienced.

In Sheola he managed, somehow, to get through the traffic until he reached the manse. He left Randy's body in the car and went into the house. Nonna met him just inside the door. She was fighting against inner agony with all the strength of her disciplined life.

"Ann has collapsed," she said. She put her arms about Paul. "Dr. Carmel is with her. We mustn't crack, darling! We've got to bear it. God will help us bear it." But she turned her face away to war with her grief.

Paul clung to her a moment, for a man never gets too old to know a time when he would cling to his mother. But he drew himself away from the comfort of her arms; he thrust her gently away and went into the bedroom. He saw Ann stretched pale and still on the bed. Dr. Carmel turned to him.

"I've given her a strong sedative," he murmured. "She'll rest for some time. I'm so sorry, Mr. Jenner."

Paul stood looking down at Ann, silent.

Carmel asked, "Where is the boy's body?"

"In the car," said Paul without looking at the doctor.

Carmel left the room quietly. Paul remained over Ann, fighting to hold his balance. A long quivering sigh expanded his lungs and emptied them. Slowly he went down on his knees and put his face against the unconscious Ann. Nonna came and knelt beside him, her arm about him, her face a mask of grief, her lips moving in an unspoken prayer.

Suddenly Paul turned and gripped Nonna's shoulders.

"When she opens her eyes, Nonna, what shall I say to her?"

"Pray that God will speak to her, darling. What you have to say to her will not be enough."

He shut his eyes tightly. "What God has to say to her may not be enough, either!" He let go of Nonna's shoulders. "If He's saying something to me I can't seem to hear it!"

"You'll be able to hear Him better after a while, Paul," Nonna said. "We'll all be able to hear Him better after a while! It's hard to hear when you hurt so much!"

Her face went down on the bed and she began to weep.

CHAPTER 19

A<small>NN DID NOT ATTEND THE FUNERAL OF HER SON.</small>

At Dr. Carmel's orders she was still lying in the hospital, her mind still fogged with sedatives, when a low-voiced minister spoke his message above the little coffin where Randy lay.

Nonna sat close to Paul during the funeral service. And on his other hand was Frances March, stiff-backed and pale, seemingly more angry than sorrowful.

Mrs. March had flown in from Grand Arbor and swept in on the scene of heartbreak, aggravating rather than assuaging it. She had a message in her looks which Paul understood though all the message was not in her words. She blamed Paul for both the death of his son as well as for the condition of her daughter. He had the feeling that she was restraining her feelings till the first woe was past; then she would instigate the second woe herself.

Paul was beyond the relief of tears. He sat unmoving while the minister spoke of a hope in a world above. A vast "why?" filled his mind. He kept hearing Randy uttering his childish words, and he thought of an old poem. *Lord, take my hand and walk; and listen to my baby talk. . . .*

With the funeral over Paul locked himself in his study.

He could not bear to watch his mother-in-law as she roamed the house, restless, angry, judgment glittering in her pale eyes.

Paul sat staring at Randy's picture on the desk. *I wonder what you would have been as a man? A minister? A doctor? A congressman . . . ?* He put out his fingers and touched the face in the picture; but he got up and went to the window to look out at Sheola. The wind was hot that came through to his face. He felt the sweat-bugs running down his chest under his shirt.

There's still the town, he thought. *Just like it was. Nothing has changed down there. Nothing is supposed to stop a man from taking the Gospel to the people who need it. Nothing.*

A knock sounded on the door that led to the church auditorium.

"Who is it?" he muttered.

"It's Carla, Paul."

He let her in and when she was seated sank into his own chair. His hair was rumpled. He did not look at Carla.

Carla said gently, "I've been praying for you, Paul. So have many in the church. And we all hurt with you, if that helps."

He lifted his eyes to her. "It helps a lot, Carla."

"I hate to trouble you, but Cal Young just phoned. He wanted to know about you. He's in a pretty desperate mood, you know. He really blames himself for what happened to Randy."

Paul nodded soberly. "I'm bothered about him. I'll see him soon and see if I can reassure him. It wasn't his fault, of course, in any sense of the word."

"Everyone seems to realize this except Cal Young."

"I know." He sighed deeply. "Carla, I want to thank you for the way you've taken charge of so many things. God bless you."

"I did what I was supposed to do, Paul. I'm only sorry I can't do more. I wish I could bear a small part of your sufferings!"

He shot a look to her and saw her tears. He let his eyes return to the floor. Silence ran in the room for a time. Then Carla spoke again, her voice tight.

"There's something else I came to tell you, Paul."

His head lifted. "Yes?"

"I just had a phone call from Dr. Carmel. . . ."

"Dr. Carmel?"

"Yes. It's about Ann."

He came to his feet. "Ann?"

He saw the expression in Carla's eyes. He cried, "I must get to the hospital."

She caught his arm. "No, Paul. Dr. Carmel said for you to wait here in the study for him. He'll be by in a few minutes. Oh, there's his car now, I think."

She went to open the door for the physician and he entered. His eyes were cloudy with gloom, his face drawn.

"Doctor!" Paul's voice was too high. "Tell me—"

The doctor's shoulders sagged. "There are times, Mr. Jenner, when I wish I were anything but a doctor. I wish—"

"What is it, doctor?"

"Mr. Jenner, I have to tell you that there won't be any little girl!"

Paul stood fettered to the floor, slowly sagging with despair. Carmel grabbed his arm.

"There's no way to lessen a blow like that, Mr. Jenner. And it seems you've had more than your share of blows lately."

Numbness seemed to lay hold on Paul's entire body. His mind seemed trying to escape from him, to escape the words he had just heard. From far inside of him someone other than himself appeared to voice a prayer.

God in heaven, we can never comfort Ann . . . now! This will be too much for her — she will die. Must everybody die?

"I think you'd better come with me to the hospital to see her, Mr. Jenner," the doctor said in his quiet voice.

He ran his hand across his eyes. "How can I see her? What can I do to help her?"

"She needs you." The physician's hand tightened on his arm, urging him toward the door. "I'll drive you in my car."

At the hospital he stared down at Ann, frightened by her thinness and whiteness. She lay with her eyes closed as if insensible to everything about her. Paul put out a trembling hand and touched her chalky cheek. Her eyes came open slowly, like curtains lifting on two stages. Her features, as she gazed up at him, were expressionless.

"Ann!" He knelt, whispering. "I'm so sorry, darling!"

Her voice was very low, as she said, "There's nothing left, is there?"

He took up her strengthless hand and put it to his mouth. He could not speak for the moment. But finally he said, "There's always God, darling."

"God?" He would always remember the way she said the one word.

He recalled how he had once told a grief-tormented mother, who had lost an only child, "There are times when even God does not seem sufficient for our human heartbreaks. But He is all we have."

Ann lay motionless for a space, then she murmured in her passionless voice, "Are we such great sinners that we must suffer so much, Paul?"

His head moved in a quick denial. "It isn't that, Ann. Jesus suffered, and He was not a sinner."

But he felt how futile his words were in her ears. There appeared no argument he could raise that would mean anything. He saw that Ann's eyes were closed again. Dr. Carmel touched him on the shoulder.

"Better let her sleep now."

He nodded, put one more look on his unstirring wife, and rose slowly to his feet. As he was leaving the hospital he met Nonna coming in.

"I think it would be better not to disturb Ann for a bit, Mrs. Jenner," said Carmel.

Carmel offered to drive them to the manse, but Nonna

had her car. When they were parked before the manse Paul said, "Nonna, I'm going to get my car and go for a drive. Do me a favor, will you? Go in and tell Ann's mother what has happened. I can't tell her. You understand, don't you?"

"I understand, son. I'll tell her."

Frances March was standing at the window, gazing out, when Nonna came into the house. Mrs. March looked around at her, but she did not speak.

"Mrs. March, Ann has had another terrible misfortune," Nonna said.

The other woman wheeled about from the window. "Misfortune?"

"There isn't going to be another child. Not now, at least."

Mrs. March's face twisted. "No!"

"Yes," said Nonna. "I'm sorry."

"In heaven's name! What else can this man do to my little daughter?"

"This man — ?"

"I mean your son. You know whom I mean!"

"Now, you listen to me, Frances March — "

"Don't you order me to listen to you, or to do anything else. I'm not constituted to take orders from people like you! I hold you in utter contempt! I despise everything about you! Yes! Your son is destroying my daughter!"

"Do you have any idea how ridiculous that charge is?"

"Your son took Ann away from me. Away from everything fine and decent and clean. He dragged her down to this dirty town. He has held her here like — well, like a prisoner — till her son died. And now —"

Nonna crossed the room and caught the other woman by both shoulders, shaking her hard.

"Hear me, Mrs. March. My son was raised to be a man. He can stand being hurt. But right now he is bearing about all a man should have to bear. You're not going to load any more burdens on him! Either keep your tongue off him — or keep away from him! Let him alone, or go back home! I mean that, Mrs. March!"

"How dare you talk to me like this?"

"I dare because I'm right! You've needed someone to talk to you like this for a long time. Not that it may do any good. It may be too late to do any good. But whether it does any good or not, just remember, don't you hurt Paul Jenner any more! Do you understand me?"

Frances March saw the light that gleamed in Nonna's eyes, and she could not look at her. She turned her head. She stumbled to the davenport and sat down, putting her face in her jeweled hands. She began to weep aloud, her shoulders shaking.

Self-pity, Nonna told herself.

She turned and went into the kitchen. She could hear Mrs. March still crying. She put some water on the stove.

All right, her mind said. *Maybe it will help her to cry. Go ahead, cry! I feel like crying, too! Sometimes there just doesn't seem to be anything to do but cry!*

Nonna sat down and let the tears come. But presently she lifted her head and began drying her eyes.

"I'll make her a cup of tea," she said aloud. "At least I can do that much for her."

CHAPTER 20

PAUL'S CAR THRUST MILES of the highway under its wheels. He drove, unaware of where he traveled, or how far. A devastating sorrow kept attacking the bastions of his mind, threatening to overwhelm them. He felt as if he drove straight into abysmal darkness, deeper and deeper.

But after a time it came to him that he was approaching the park where he and Ann, with Randy, had gone for picnics several times. He halted his car and began walking through the park. Somewhere a robin made his tiny flute cry, and the sound knifed him like sharp steel.

He came to a picnic table and sat down. Then he realized it was the same table where he had sat with Ann when she had voiced her premonition that tragedy would befall them if they remained in Sheola.

The days in his past began to crowd in upon him, asking to be reviewed. And his mind examined some of them.

You were so beautiful, Ann, when we met in Grand Arbor that first time. So like some rare tender blossom. I knew I'd always love you. How I wanted to keep you from all hurt, all pain! And what pain you have known, what grief! I'm so sorry, darling. Please get well, live, walk in the sun with me again, love me — and we'll both live again! We can live again, baby — even with little Randy gone. Can't we?

Randy!

You didn't seem so extraordinary when I first saw you. Just a tiny little thing, all helpless, without too much personality, until I saw you looking at me, that is, with those eyes I learned to look into so often. The doctor said you couldn't see at that age, but I never quite believed him! The eyes of my son, looking at me!

Something happened to me. A new world sprang open. A world that some men never know. I used to go about feeling sorry for men like that.

How fast you grew! Is there anything in our world like the development of a baby? I watched the miracle until perhaps I almost took the miracle for granted. And I never knew how soon the miracle would be taken from me.

The way you came to my heart, nearer and nearer, action by action, sound by sound, smile by smile, till you had moved into the heart, and made a home there; how proud I felt because you had moved in! Day after day hundreds of little things were happening to you, things making an impact on your inner soul. And so many things happened that you would never consciously remember, that I could never quite forget.

Oh, you needed me, but I needed you, too. You caused me to realize a little better how much I needed God.

Those mornings when you always woke in your crib before either Ann or I wakened, and you stood up, laughing at nothing, save the wild joy of being alive!

How you crawled across the floor before your legs would bear you up; and when I went from one room to another, there you came, scooting incredibly fast after me. You caught my trouser legs and pulled yourself up, and you kept looking up at me, till there was nothing to do but stoop and lift you up. With what gloating contentment you settled in the curve of my arm, riding high. It was all pretty wonderful, little fellow.

Your first wobbly step, when you left your crawling

stage for keeps, and the Caesar-like look as you accomplished it!

Your first word! And the uncanny way you added to your vocabulary day after day.

One day I looked, and you were a miniature man! A little man walking, standing a little past knee-high to me. And it seemed, by then, I had known you forever. There had never been a time in the world when I had not known you.

And the words of Jesus came home to me once with great power. *My Father and I are one!*

Then . . . you were gone!

And part of me was gone.

Paul swayed slightly on the picnic-table seat. But all at once he lifted his eyes to the heavens. He cried in silence, God's Son died, too, and they were still One! Death did not alter their oneness.

He stood up and spoke aloud, "Randy . . . we are still part of each other, somehow. Time, distance, even death, cannot change that. In God's world we are still part of each other, and in God's time, and His place, we shall be together again!

He felt the tears like fire in his eyes, but he knew he had his crucifixion licked; there was a sound of a grievous tomb cracking open in his soul.

He drove back to Sheola with his spirits lifted higher than they had been for several days. He was parking in front of the manse when his brother parked behind him and got out of his car.

Matt said, "I didn't come to the funeral, Paul. I knew Young would be there, and I couldn't trust myself in his presence. Not after he killed little Randy!"

"If you're going to keep on as a fool, Matt, I'd rather not see you!" cried Paul.

"Oh, I know. He's still good Saint Cal to you. But he's added one more Jenner to his list of killings!"

"I'm not listening to you, Matt. Go away."

"You don't think Young would do that, do you? You don't believe he's really a murderer at heart. He's killed your father, and your son, and you still want him for a brother!"

"How much do you think I can take from you, Matt?"

"Okay. I'm sorry you've been hurt, and I mean that. But you've asked for some of it, man! You'd better take another look at that killer in your flock!"

Paul gave a groan. Matt wheeled and tramped to his car. When he had driven away Paul started his car and drove to Young's apartment.

Young, tired-looking, unsmiling, motioned him toward a chair.

Paul said, "Cal, I know this thing has been tough on you."

"I'll never get over it, Paul," Young said in a strained tone. "I'm really to blame. I should have been more careful. I feel guilty —"

"Look, Cal. Right now I need your help. Don't conk out on me by torturing yourself."

"I can't get it out of my mind. I can't help how I feel about it."

"You're not just a man I'm acquainted with, Cal. I think I know you well enough to know you'd rather have died yourself than to have this thing happen to Randy."

Young swallowed hard, nodded. He said in a choked voice, "It's so, Paul. Before God, it's so."

"I've got another burden, Cal. Ann isn't going to have a baby!"

Young stiffened, groaned. "Oh, no, Paul! No!"

"It's true. But I've done some thinking today, Cal. God had a Son who died, too. Today I felt God was hurting *with* me! It helps more than anything I know."

Young put his hand on Paul's shoulder. "It must be like that, Paul. He *must* hurt with us."

"I suppose a man has to stagger when he's hit hard. I've been staggering, and so have you. But what matters is how soon we can get our feet under us again and start walking."

Young inhaled deeply, and let his breath out. He moved to press Paul's shoulders. "You've lost a son, Paul. I never had one. Would you mind being my son?"

Paul suddenly felt tired. He turned his eyes on Young's face, a quiet smile about his lips. "I don't mind, Cal. It sounds all right."

CHAPTER 21

ANN CAME HOME FROM THE HOSPITAL. Her pale fragility unnerved Paul. He thought of a white lily crushed in someone's hand and tossed away. Her illness wasn't merely physical, of course. Much of it lay deep in her tormented spirit. Most of the time she was uncommunicative. Her face had an emptiness that Paul had never dreamed would be there.

Frances March was also quite uncommunicative. She did not berate Paul to his face again; in fact she ignored him most ot the time, as well as she did Nonna. She spent a great deal of time with her daughter.

Paul attempted again and again to break through his wife's taciturnity, but he did not succeed. Ann had locked herself in prison and she would not surrender the key.

But finally Paul did get her to talk. They were alone in the bedroom one evening and he said, "You must find a way to drop the past, darling. It's not an easy thing to do, I know! But it has to be done. You will keep remembering with your heart, perhaps, but your mind must forget. You understand, don't you?"

Ann's head stirred in a negation. "No, I don't understand."

"Ann, honey, I've had to fight with my own soul. I realize what you're suffering."

"I had two children," said Ann. "I had two wonderful children. Now I have none."

Paul almost said, "You had one child, Ann." But he didn't. Ann was a woman; she had lost two children. Paul put his arms tenderly about her thin body.

"Our loss is great, sweetheart. Will we lose each other also?"

She drew away from him, her slim shoulders drooping. He reached to touch her again, but took back his hand. He could nearly hear her thinking, struggling with her thoughts. She turned slowly back to him.

"Paul, I'm going to leave!"

His eyes stared on her with incredulity. "Leave?"

"I'm going to leave Sheola. I'm going home with Mother for a — while. I can't stay here any longer. I can't bear it. I must go away and see if I can forget what has happened to me — to us — in Sheola."

He considered her words. "Do you really wish to go?"

"It's the best thing for me, Paul."

His shoulders fell. "All right, Ann."

"Why don't you come with me, Paul? You need a long rest. The weather is cooler in Michigan. It's so hot here, so dusty."

His head moved. "No, Ann. I can't leave. I am too involved in my work here to forsake it now. I could go with you to Michigan, but I'd have to come right back. I belong here."

"Why couldn't someone else take the church?"

"Someone else?"

"It's really too difficult a charge, Paul. There are other churches, in better places. Churches far better than this. We could stay with Mother until you were rested up — then we could look for another place."

"Haven't I told you, Ann? I feel it is God's will for me to pastor here! I can't walk out on a charge simply because it is difficult. Don't you know that?"

"It seems there is so much about you I don't understand, Paul. Why do you think it's more Christian to keep on in a heart-breaking charge rather than one that offers you more success in the church?"

"Haven't I explained it, darling? I am convinced that God wants me in Sheola. As much as Livingstone knew he was needed in Africa! A Christian is a soldier. Ours is to carry out orders, not to ask for specific appointments that might be easier for us!"

She dropped down wearily on the bed. Her hands were small and pale against her orchid house-dress.

"I don't feel like a soldier. There's no fight in me. I have no strength for fighting."

He sat down beside her, folding a cold hand in his own. "Very well. It may be best for you to go to Grand Arbor for a good rest. I shall be praying for you, every day. God will restore you. Then you'll come back to me. And we'll carry on together again."

She did not reply to this and her very silence put a chill deep inside him.

In the next two days Ann prepared to take her trip. Paul was aware of the gleam of triumph in the eyes of Frances March. She seemed a changed person. She even appeared quite friendly to Paul at times. But she maintained her coldness toward Nonna whenever the latter visited the manse.

But on the morning the two were ready to leave for the airport in Tulsa, Mrs. March caught Nonna apart from the others for a moment.

"Before I go," she said icily, "I just want to tell you that you are nothing but an arrogant peasant!"

Nonna's eyes flashed, but she refused to reply to the insult. She turned away, and as she turned Mrs. March cried, "And your son is not one whit better!"

Nonna walked away from her in utter silence.

Paul drove Ann and her mother to the Tulsa airport, Nonna accompanying them. Ann kissed Paul good-by without apparent feeling. She boarded the plane, looking back to wave feebly. The plane raged away and grew smaller and smaller in the sky to the north, till it was gone. Paul turned slowly to Nonna.

"I wish I didn't feel what I do!"

Nonna nodded. "I know."

"She isn't coming back, Nonna!" There was an agony in his throat.

"I don't know, Paul. She would come back — if it wasn't for her mother!"

"But she'll see to it that she stays away from me. Ann can't break her chains. I thought for a while she was free of them — but she isn't. What will I do now, Nonna?"

"I don't know that, either, son. I just don't know. But I know you'll do what you're supposed to do. I've known you'd do it since you were a small child."

"Don't be too sure, Nonna!"

"Oh, I have to be sure! I haven't much else to be sure about, except my faith in God. My husband failed me. One of my sons let me down utterly. My daughter-in-law ran out on me. You're about all I have, Paul, to prove to myself that life can be bigger than any of its oppositions!"

He laid a hand on her shoulder. "God bless you, Nonna. I'll do my best."

That night sleep escaped him. The flower-like face of Ann floated before him in the darkness. And when he sank into a half-sleep he saw little Randy standing in his crib laughing at him. He got up and took the crib into another room. Back in bed sleep still fled him. He rose and wandered about the house. The emptiness of the place smote him as a shock.

Maybe I should have let Nonna stay tonight, as she wished, he thought.

When sleep finally came, toward dawn, he heard Randy crying for help. And he saw Ann standing at a distance, saying, "He can't help us, Randy. Nobody can help any of us!"

He awakened, soaked with sweat. He lay back, breathing a prayer. But sleep did not come again. A muggy gray dawn was nagging the windows. He lay thinking.

How smugly we set up our little formulas for a happy life! How easily we lay down all the little program, saying, do this, don't do this, and all will be well with you! And how we lie to ourselves! Telling ourselves that life can be always beautiful, if we'd only have it so! Oh, life can be ugly! Life can be deadly! Jordan *can* be a hard road to travel, as the old song says. Why do we keep trying to make ourselves believe our soft sentiments, to keep forever trying to make the way always rosy and dreamy and smooth?

Life has a cross in it. That's what Jesus said about it. And the cross is ugly. It is a gangster's stick! The only reason it's beautiful is because a Man was spread-eagled on it, a Man who was dedicated to deliver humanity from death. *There* is the real beauty, a soul consecrated to the business of taking ugliness and making it lovely by the surrender of himself to such a mission. There is a wonder in a God-made spirit, clothed in the armor of grace, not only enduring against all evil, but prevailing over it, even with the terrible shape of a cross. . . .

He pulled himself out of bed. He must get a sermon on what he had been thinking. He left the bedroom and went into the kitchen. He made coffee. He did not cook any food for he knew he could not eat. He drank the coffee and went into his study. He jotted down some ideas for his new sermon. But he was in no mood to continue with the message. He knelt down by his desk and began to pray.

Sometime later there was a knock at the door. It was Carla with a sheaf of letters for his signature. He signed them swiftly. He looked up at Carla.

"Ann's gone!" he said simply.

"I heard. How long will she stay?" asked Carla.

He frowned, winced slightly. "I don't know."

She watched his face and said, "Paul, I've been thinking you could use a long rest yourself."

"Maybe. But that will have to wait. Right now I need work more than I need rest."

"I suppose so. What can I do to make things easier for you?"

He spread his hands. "You've already done more than you'd ever be expected to do."

"I have a lot of vitality. I can take it."

"You really can. In fact, you're rather wonderful!"

She started to smile, but the smile faded. "Never talk to me like that, Paul!"

His mouth pursed. "Why?"

"You know why. Don't tell me I'm wonderful, or pretty, or anything like that!"

Stillness enveloped the room until his voice broke through it. "All right, Carla."

Her mouth tightened; her look on him was direct. "You know how I feel about you, don't you?"

He sat very still. "I wish you hadn't said that, Carla! Will everything be different now?"

"Paul, I am aware of your determination to serve God and the church. And I know something else. I know how you love Ann! I am a fool for feeling as I do toward you. The best thing I can do is to leave this job immediately!"

He was on his feet. "Carla, listen. We are people who believe in something. We teach a strong Gospel. We say that God's grace can make us what we should be. If we crack people will say we couldn't stand the pressure of life. But we both know it's a lie to say we can't stand the pressure! We know we can! Maybe it isn't easy, but people can live in this world without violating the principles of right and decency. Am I right?"

"Why must you say all this to me?"

"Don't you know why, Carla? Don't walk out on me! I need you!"

"But, Paul — "

"With Ann out of the picture I might easily pursue you, and you know it! But you also know Ann isn't out of the picture — not in *my* heart, at least! As for you, I've said you were a wonderful person. But you're a Christian. So am I. We've got to act like Christians! First, last, and in between. No matter what happens! Okay?"

Carla was pale. "You only make me care more for you!

Don't you know what a woman admires in a man?''

"I am flattered, Carla. I almost feel heroic! But I have a real faith in you, in your ability to come through as a believer. You won't crack. Still, I'm asking a lot of you; I know that. So if you want to run, run! I won't ever blame you. Only I wish you'd stay and help me lick my problems!''

She stood unstirring, unspeaking. She looked away from his intense eyes. The silence continued. But at last he broke it. "What about it, Carla? Or do you need time to think it over?''

"You ask a lot of me, you say. You ask more than you know. But I am rather stuck with your regard for my ability to carry on as a Christian! I can't let you down, I guess!''

"Thank you, Carla. And God bless you.''

Carla went to the door and out. Paul took in a sharp breath, studying the door through which she had passed. He put his head down and prayed. *Dear Lord, I thank Thee that there are still people in the world like her!*

A sound at the other study door drew his attention. Nonna came in. She smiled rather sheepishly at Paul.

"I was embarrassed to come in. The study door was not quite closed, and I just couldn't help hearing the conversation.''

"Oh?''

"It was one of the most interesting conversations I've ever eavesdropped on!''

"You think so?''

"You know what I was afraid of when I heard her say she cared for you? I thought, 'My soul, now I've got to get hold of that girl and put her straight! I've got to show her what she must do! And I've got to get hold of Paul and see if I can get more iron into him!' That's what I thought.''

"Hmmmm.''

"Well, it's heart-warming to find people who can manage their lives without an old woman butting in! I wanted to stand out there and yell, 'Hurrah!' When you made that speech, I mean. That was about the finest sermon I ever heard you deliver, son. And there you were standing back of the sermon, making it work. I'm glad I went to the trouble of raising a son like you!''

He lifted his hand. ''I already feel a little vain about my goodness, Nonna! Don't make me into a real Pharisee!''

CHAPTER 22

THE WEATHER WAS PLEASANT in Grand Arbor. It was neither too hot nor too cool. It had rained last night and there was a fresh-washed smell to the earth.

Ann sat in a deck chair on the huge porch of her mother's great white house. The spacious yard stretching out to the street was very green. Bright shrubbery and flowers stood along the curving driveway that led up to the porch.

Ann's face was less thin than when she had left Sheola. Her face was also darkened from a good tan. Arrayed in a pink dress she leaned back in the comfortable chair, her eyes closed. Tiny parts of the past sprang across her mind like quick sentences remembered from an old book.

Little Randy jabbered countless questions as he tugged at her dress.

The glow she had known when she promised Randy and Paul a baby daughter and sister.

The terror of knowing that Randy was no longer alive.

The look in Paul's eyes as she took the plane for Michigan.

In the midst of her thoughts Frances March came out on

the porch and sat near Ann. She said, "Did I disturb your thinking, baby?"

Ann did not open her eyes or turn her head. "I'm afraid you did!"

"Oh? What were you thinking about?"

"You wouldn't want to know, perhaps."

"Of course I would, darling. I always want to know what my baby is thinking about."

"Well, for one thing I was thinking about Paul."

"That's but natural, dear. You'll think about him many times no doubt."

Ann's eyes opened. "Mother, I was wrong to leave him!"

"Wrong? What else was there to do, darling?"

"I might have stayed and stood with him. I ran out on him! I'm a coward!"

"Now, baby. We've been through all that before. You were ill, terribly ill. You would have died if you had stayed in that dirty place. I'm positive of that. You did the only sensible thing you could do when you left."

Ann sat upright. "But I love him, Mother! And I know he still loves me."

"Does he really love you, Ann?"

"Yes!"

"How many letters have you written him?"

"I don't know — several."

"I should know! I mailed all of them for you. You must have written him a dozen times at least. And how many answers have you received?"

"None — but he's so busy — "

She hesitated at her lame words. To herself Mrs. March was thinking, *I must never let her know that I never mailed her letters – or that I intercepted his letters to her. Or that I told him when he phoned that Ann was not here!*

Aloud she said, "And you still maintain that he loved you? When a man loves a woman he should do something about it. If he *really* loved you, Ann, he'd leave that dreadful place and come here to live with you."

"But his work is there."

"Darling, he doesn't *have* to work there. There are many other places where he could work. Don't you realize that he wants to force you to his will, to drag you down there, in spite of the fact he knows you can't endure such a hole?"

Ann was silent for a time, her lips compressed. Then she said, "Mother, Paul is a true Christian. I believe that with all my heart. That's why he undergoes hardships for the Lord and for the church."

"Have you ever considered the fact that he may be a fanatic? Many men have suffered untold miseries for wrong principles just because they were fanatical."

"Tell me something, Mother. Are you a Christian?"

Mrs. March probed her daughter with pale eyes. "How can you ask such a question? Of course I'm a Christian! I've always been a Christian."

"Always?"

"Certainly. I have attended church for as far back as I can remember. I have always been religious. I've never indulged in the wicked stupidities of so many people. Why, I've never so much as drunk a cocktail in my life! Though I've attended many cocktail parties. I haven't even smoked a cigarette in my life! I've always been a Christian. And so have you, my dear."

Ann's head movement denied her mother's words. "You're wrong, Mother!"

"Wrong?"

"I wasn't always a Christian! I can remember well when I became a Christian."

"What are you talking about, darling?"

"I was about seven, I think. One Sunday morning a tall minister spoke in our church, a visiting minister — I don't remember his name. He spoke about God's grace, I remember that so well. I don't even recall his text. But I recall his sermon made a terrific impact on my young heart. The words stayed with me all that Sunday, and the next day. Finally, when I got to bed Monday night, I began to pray. To *really* pray, I mean. Oh, I had repeated prayers which I learned in babyhood; but this night I prayed a prayer I had never learned. I wasn't just repeating something. I was praying right out of my heart, speaking directly to God — and He was listening to me! And it came to me that Jesus was *actually* the Mediator — though at the time I didn't know the word — the Mediator between God and sinful humanity — ''

"Baby, I don't — ''

"I felt how wrong sin was! I knew I was in need of a Saviour! But God heard my prayer. I can't explain it, but a sweet glow came to me, filled my soul. I seemed to be in another world, and it was wonderful, wonderful! It left me wanting to weep and sing both. It was indescribable!''

Ann paused and her mother gazed at her in amazement. "Why on earth didn't you tell me about all this — then?''

"I did.''

"You *did?*''

"I told you the very next morning.''

"What are you saying?''

"I tried to tell you, I mean. I wanted so much for you to know. But you said I was too young for such things. You said, 'Please don't bother your sweet little head about such things!' ''

"I don't remember any of this.''

"I have never forgotten. Always afterward when I heard the minister read from the Bible I felt something wonderful was being given to the world. The feeling I had that Monday night came back to me again and again, through the years.''

"The impressions of childhood have a way of clinging to us, my dear.''

"That was more than a childhood impression. It was an experience in my inner being. It was a wonderful thing.''

"Oh, look!'' cried Mrs. March. "Here comes Ronald Ferren!''

A sky-blue Cadillac purred up the curved driveway and stopped, and a tall, good-looking man in a gray suit got out. The man carried himself in the manner of one born to plenty and to elegance. His crew-cut dark hair was hatless; a habitual smile crinkled the skin about his brown eyes. His tan was deep.

"Why hello, Ronald," said Mrs. March. "Please come in."

Ronald Ferren came up on the porch. He smiled his greeting to Ann, his eyes lingering on her.

"You're looking wonderful, Ann," he said.

"Thank you, Mr. Ferren."

"Oh, come now, Ann," he said. "You've known me long enough to call me Ronald. Don't you agree, Mrs. March?"

"I was thinking the same thing," was the reply.

Ferren kept his eyes on Ann while he sat to talk with them. Ann looked away from him; but when she glanced at him again she discovered he was eyeing her closely.

"I dropped by to extend to each of you a personal invitation to attend a party I'm giving for the church choir in my home next Monday evening."

"You are very kind, Ronald," said Mrs. March quickly. "We'll be happy to attend."

"Neither of you belong to the choir, of course. But I'd like you to come as my special guests." His eyes gave Ann the special invitation.

"That's so sweet of you," murmured Mrs. March.

Ann started to say something, but Ferren was talking to Mrs. March, and she desisted. When Ferren had departed Mrs. March sighed deeply. "He's such a charming young man! He's awfully wealthy, too! And, oh, how eligible!" She put her hand on Ann's arm. "If only you had waited, darling!"

"Oh, Mother, please!"

"It may not be too late yet, you know!"

Ann came to her feet at once. She went to the door, turned. "You accepted the invitation, not I!"

"Let's not be like that, baby. You'll have a wonderful time. Just wait and see."

"Will I?"

Ann went upstairs to her room. It was a lovely room,

done in pink. A few minutes later she heard the phone ring in the hall. She went out to answer it but heard her mother speaking in answer downstairs. She returned to her room.

Downstairs Mrs. March heard a girl's voice speaking. "This is Sheola, Oklahoma, calling for Mrs. Paul Jenner. Is this Mrs. Jenner?"

Mrs. March pitched her low voice. "No. Mrs. Jenner is not here."

"Hello, sir," said the operator. "Mrs. Jenner is not at home. Will you speak with someone else at this number?"

"I'll speak to Mrs. March," said Paul Jenner's voice.

The operator asked Mrs. March if she were Mrs. March. Then she said, "Go ahead, sir."

"Mrs. March?" said Paul. "This is Paul. I want to speak to Ann."

A cold smile creased the corners of the mouth of Frances March. The expression that a gambler might have when he bet everything he had in one gesture stood in her eyes.

"Ann isn't here. She's on a date with — Ronald Ferren!"

"A date? With *who?*"

"Mr. Ferren. You wouldn't know him."

There was a sudden stillness at the other end of the line. Then Paul said, in a hoarse tone, "Mrs. March, will you tell Ann I phoned, when she comes in, and tell her I asked her to call me?"

"Why, yes, of course. But I'm afraid it will be very late. She usually stays out late when she goes out with Ronald."

There was a click in Sheola.

Mrs. March smiled to herself. She went back to the porch. She spoke to herself aloud, "How nice it would be to have a man like Ronald Ferren in the family!"

After Ann had gone to bed that night Mrs. March went to the phone again. She spoke softly into the mouthpiece.

"Hello. Western Union? I'd like to send a night letter, please."

CHAPTER 23

IT WAS PAST MIDNIGHT. Nonna had been visiting Paul at the manse, and she started to go home earlier, but he had asked her to stay.

Paul said in a strained voice, "She's out late with him, Nonna. I hope now that she doesn't call at all. I don't think I could talk to her . . . after she's been out with another man."

"It's difficult for me to believe it has really come to this!" Nonna's face was agitated. "It seems impossible — that she should be going out with another man, so soon after she left here. And so soon after little Randy's death!"

Paul's body sagged against the davenport. "I never dreamed — Nonna, do you have any idea how much I love her?"

Nonna came and sat beside him, touching him. "I think I do. If only there was something we could do about it. Perhaps you should go and see her, Paul."

"When a woman wants another man what is there to do about it? Nonna, didn't I try? Didn't I treat her as a man should treat his wife? Tell me the truth, Nonna."

"I've never used flattery on you, Paul. I won't do it

148

now. You're a fine husband! I'd put you up against any of them!"

"Then why does she hate me?"

"I can't believe that she hates you, Paul. She's frustrated, confused, yes. And her mother isn't helping her, of course. But I refuse to think she hates you. It might be good if you went to see her."

He shook his head. "I can't do that! I've written. I've phoned. She doesn't want to contact me. If I went up and persuaded her to come back with me I'd never be satisfied. I'd always wonder if she *really* wanted to return. No, she must make her own decision!" He shut his eyes tightly and opened them. "And it looks like she may have made it!"

"Perhaps I'll begin to sound trite, darling. But we must trust in God. I'm still old-fashioned enough to believe in miracles!"

His breath came out quickly. "Looks like I could use one!"

"Shall I stay here tonight, dear?"

He made a gesture. "No. I'd rather be alone. You understand, don't you?"

"Of course. I'll run along, then. I'll get in touch with you first thing in the morning. If she calls, you can tell me about it then — if you feel like it."

When his mother had gone Paul began to walk about the house. In the kitchen he recalled how Ann had looked standing at the stove in a clean apron. He went into the bedroom and saw Randy's picture on the dresser. He took it up and pressed it against his cheek. Tears glittered in his eyes.

Looks like she's walked out on us, cowboy . . .

Ann's picture struck his eyes from the other side of the dresser. He put Randy's picture down and reached toward Ann's, but his hand came back without touching it.

What happened, Ann? Where did we get lost from each other?

He returned to the living room, but he could not sit down. He had decided Ann wasn't going to call. Perhaps it was to escape her call, if it came, that he went out into the street and began to walk. It was two o'clock when he got back from walking.

In his bed, in the dark, he began wondering what Ronald Ferren was like. He wondered what Ann was saying to him, what he was saying to her. He saw Ferren bend to kiss her, and a knife twisted inside him. He sat up with a groan, his throat too tight for breathing. He quit his bed and began to wander about the house again.

At last he went to the phone and dialed a number. After a while a sleepy-voiced Cal Young said, "Hello."

"You said you wanted to be my father, Cal. Well, I think I need one pretty badly. Do you have any idea how a father should pray for a son, if the son was getting really kicked into the dirt?"

"Paul! What is it?"

"Just pray for me. I need help from heaven!"

"Hold everything, Paul. I'll be over in a few minutes."

"No, Cal. That wouldn't help. Just pray for me. All right?"

"All right, Paul. You can count on it. Should I know what the trouble is?"

"I'll tell you about it tomorrow."

"Okay. God bless you."

He hung up and after meandering about for another hour he finally lay down again. He prayed for a long time. Then he tossed and fought with his mind. He prayed some more. At five o'clock he dozed off into a world of crazy dreams. He was startled awake by the ringing of the phone.

"This is Western Union, Mr. Jenner. I have a long night letter for you. It's rather long to read over the phone. Shall I send it out?"

"Send it out," he said, wondering who could be sending him a long night letter.

When the messenger brought the wire he ripped it open. He read it quickly, and sat down. He stood up again, his breath whistling into his lungs. He read the wire once more.

PAUL, I AM WIRING YOU BECAUSE I DO NOT
WISH TO ARGUE WITH YOU ON THE PHONE.
PLEASE DO NOT TRY TO CALL ME AGAIN. I AM
VERY HAPPY HERE. MY HEART INTERESTS AT
PRESENT ARE BETTER UNMOLESTED. THINGS CAN
NEVER BE RIGHT WITH US AGAIN. WE HAD OUR
OPPORTUNITY AND THINGS DID NOT WORK OUT.
OUR WORLDS JUST AREN'T THE SAME. THEY
NEVER CAN BE. PLEASE BE KIND TO ME AND LET
ME LIVE MY LIFE AS I CHOOSE. WE WILL ARRANGE
THINGS LEGALLY LATER. IN THE MEANTIME
ALLOW ME THE RIGHT TO FOLLOW MY OWN
HEART. PLEASE DO THIS FOR ME, WILL YOU?

ANN

Half-way through the telegram for the third time he
suddenly wadded it up and hurled it on the floor.

She-Demas! You rotten little She-Demas!

He was shaking as a rag in the wind. He was still
shaking when the doorbell rang. He hesitated, then strode
and flung the door open. It was Carla Brown.

"I wanted to talk to you — " she said. Then she cried,
"Paul! What on earth is wrong?"

He grinned with no hint of mirth. He picked up the
telegram and unballed it, handing it to her. "You'll know
anyhow in time," he muttered.

Carla read it, her face showing her perturbation. "Oh,
no! She couldn't!"

"Oh, she couldn't, huh?"

He wheeled and walked into the kitchen. She followed
him. "Paul . . . you'll have to get hold of yourself!"

"Will I?" The bitterness in his voice made her wince.

"There's the church to think of — "

He swung toward her, his blue-green eyes glowing.
"Sure! The church! How will I ever explain this thing to the
church? You know as well as I do what the church thinks of
divorces — especially where ministers are concerned."

"You won't have to give her a divorce!"

He stood staring at her. "Hang on to her, you mean —
when she wants another man? Don't be ridiculous! You said

151

there's the church. There *goes* the church, you mean!"

"The church loves you, Paul. You've done so much for all of us — "

"Fine! And now they'll turn and rend me! When I'm on my knees like a beat-up pug, when I'm trying to keep from going down for the count!"

"You don't mean that, Paul. You're hurt — badly. But you don't mean it."

He ran his trembling fingers through his hair. His eyes were bloodshot from lack of sleep. He needed a shave.

"All right," he mumbled, "maybe I don't mean it."

"I know you don't."

"But I'm finished as a minister."

"You're not finished. You'll never be finished. Not if I have to spend the rest of my life fighting for you!"

His gaze clung to her. He tried to smile. "I told you you were wonderful. Remember?"

"Never mind me. We have to think about you right now."

"I'm something to think about, that's for sure."

"Yes, you certainly are!"

He put his look on the floor, then on her again. "I suppose the first thing to do is call the elders of the church together and tell them their pastor has just lost a wife — the hard way! First a son, then a wife. And, God help me, it was easier to lose the son!"

"You mustn't be bitter!"

"Of course not! I must be sweet and noble. I must smile gently at the world and say, 'Peace, it's wonderful!' "

"Irony! It's good for your soul. Keep it up! I think the Lord is helping you!"

"Ha!" He set his mouth. "One thing Ann should know. I still have Carla Brown on my side! That might make her take notice! A woman who has the stuff to fight when the going gets really rough. She probably never knew a woman like that in all her life — "

He stopped. His eyes burned with tears. She smiled faintly. "I don't think you'd better call in the elders, yet.

Wait a while. You can tell your mother and Cal Young, and I already know. We won't make this thing public yet."

"What do you mean? Do you imagine you can keep a juicy scandal like this quiet?"

"When its gets too noisy we'll call in the elders. Meantime, you mustn't discount God! He's still working on your case, you know!"

He frowned, rubbed his hand over his unshaven chin. "Yes. Thanks for reminding me, Carla."

"You're welcome. We'll just let things run along for the present. Okay?"

He nodded, and she went to the door, turned, smiling faintly. "Do it like Jacob at Jabbok, preacher! Remember what a fine sermon you have on that incident? Wrestle it out with God! You may get hurt, you may even come out limping, as Jacob did. But you'll come out on top — and with new strength!"

When the door closed behind her a half-smile moved over his grief-stricken features. He dabbed at a wetness on his cheek with his finger.

"Some woman!" he said aloud.

CHAPTER **24**

On Sunday morning Ann accompanied her mother to the church which she had attended as a child. The regular minister was on his vacation and a young man filled the pulpit. He was rather awkward but much in earnest. He seemed unaware that he was addressing a congregation that was not used to his simple, direct way of preaching.

As the young minister compared the church to an army Ann recalled that Paul had often done the same thing.

"In Korea," said the young minister, "I knew a captain whose own son was in his regiment. One day he ordered his son on a mission that was pretty sure to mean death for the son. The boy took his orders, made no argument, saluted. He went out and died."

The speaker paused, then said, "Must we forever keep asking the great Commander, 'Why?' when He orders us to fulfill our mission for Him? When will we come to say, 'Thy will be done'?"

His words were sharp in Ann's ears. Her mind said, *Paul is like that soldier! He takes his orders and carries them out, at whatever cost!* Tears were fire-drops in her eyes.

The following afternoon Frances March bustled about in preparation for attending Ronald Ferren's choir party.

"Mother," Ann said, "I don't really want to go to the party."

"Oh, Ann, dear!" cried Mrs. March. "Must you spoil everything for me? After I've counted so much on going?"

"Couldn't you go alone? I just don't feel like a party."

Mrs. March grew very solemn, very sad. "Then I will not go, either. Much as I'd love to. I can't run off and leave you here, knowing how alone you'll be — after all the things you've been through!"

At last Ann surrendered to her mother's wishes and agreed to attend the party.

Ronald Ferren's house was in keeping with his wealth. It was even larger than Frances March's house. It was located in that area of Grand Arbor that people called exclusive, for here resided the elite. The imposing building stood far back from the boulevard among great trees. The yard was surrounded by a high stone fence. The entrance to the grounds was through a tall iron gate.

"Isn't this place divine?" said Mrs. March as she and Ann came to the front door.

"It's big," said Ann.

Mrs. March paused before pressing the doorbell. "Darling, most of the unmarried women in Grand Arbor would give anything for a smile from Ronald Ferren!"

"I suppose some of the *married* ones would, too!" Ann said.

"Ann, darling, must you talk like that? And, dear, you seem so *listless!* Why, you practically ooze enervation! You just must have some fun tonight. How long has it been since you had any fun?"

"Did I ever have any fun, Mother?"

"How silly you sound! Why, you were the gayest little girl in Grand Arbor! Everybody said so. And you'll be gay again, after you get over those horrible years you lost. You'll see."

But Ann's mind was on something she had heard Paul

Jenner say the first time she had ever heard him addressing a group. He had said it when he spoke to the young people where she met him. The sentence had been coming back to her for several days now, over and over.

Paul had said, "There's nothing big, good, worthwhile, but what there's a little Calvary in it!"

"Come, baby," murmured her mother.

Inside Ferren's big house they were in a vast living room. There were several guests already present. Most of them knew Ann and her mother and they greeted them. When Ronald Ferren saw them he hurried forward.

"Welcome to my domicile, pilgrims," he said lightly, his eyes taking in Ann with a glow. "Welcome, and be mirthful!"

"You're cute, Ronald!" said Mrs. March.

He glanced at her, then back to Ann. "Is she right about that, Ann?"

Ann flushed. "Are you suggesting my mother could be wrong about something?"

"Oh, not at all, princess! But it's you I want some word from. A hamburger from you would be far better than a *filet mignon* from any other!"

The man's flippancy irritated Ann immensely. She was relieved when other guests came and he excused himself to greet them.

Mrs. March whispered to Ann. "He's mad about you!"

"More likely he's just mad!"

"Ann! Be careful what you say!"

Suddenly Ann felt as irritated at her mother as she did at Ronald Ferren.

As the evening wore away Ann found herself more and more regretful that she had come to the party. The party had been given in honor of a church choir, and it was a religious group, but it appeared void of any spiritual significance. There was a constant gabble of voices, and nobody seemed to be saying anything important. One lanky young man came to Ann and said, "Democracy marches on!" He grinned broadly as if he had discovered a vast joke. Ann turned away from his fatuous grin and the young man shrugged and muttered, "I'm froze!"

Ronald Ferren kept trying to corner Ann and at last he managed it.

"Listen, princess, we must have a long talk. Just you and I. How about a stroll in my garden? Did anyone ever tell you what a lovely garden I have, just back of the house?"

Ann said coolly, "I don't care for gardens at night!"

"You don't like gardens at night? You can't mean that, princess! Why, gardens at night are out of this world! They smell like the nectar of the gods!"

There was a Man once in a garden! And at night!

"Princess, I have flowers from Asia, from Africa, and from South America — "

There was a Man in a garden, on His knees, sweating blood-drops, and the world didn't know, or care!

" — if you come into my garden I think you will change your mind." Ferren's voice now had a coaxing quality.

She put a clear look on him. "I've already changed my mind!"

"Oh, you have? That's gorgeous! Let's go, then!"

"I've changed my mind, but not about your garden."

"No? Then about what, princess?"

"I don't think you'd understand if I told you."

"Tell me, princess. Do you feel all right?"

"I feel terrible! But maybe I'll feel better after a while. If God will help me!"

"I don't think I know what you mean — "

Ann whirled and went swiftly to her mother. "Will you take me home, Mother?"

"Home, darling? We just got here!"

"All right, I'll walk!" Ann started for the door and Ferren caught up with her.

"Whatever on earth is wrong, princess?"

Ann thrust back from him. "If you call me princess once more I'll scream loud enough to break up this party!"

She went outside, grateful for the cool night air. Mrs.

March followed her outside.

"Ann, dearest. What is wrong with you?"

"I don't feel like explaining just now. Go on and have a good time with your friends. Maybe Mr. Ferren will call *you* princess! I'm leaving."

"Now, Ann, baby. You must listen to your mother."

"I've done that far too long!"

"What? What are you saying, darling?"

Ann began walking down the long curving driveway toward the iron gate. Her mother cried after her. "Do you realize it's three miles home?"

"I can walk three miles. I can walk ten! I feel as if I might walk forever!"

"Ann! You must be ill. Wait — I'll phone Doctor Marshall."

"Doctor Marshall couldn't do anything for my case. It will take a better Doctor!"

Ann kept on walking, her mother calling after her. She walked through the iron gate and took the sidewalk west. She was still walking briskly when her mother caught up with her in her car.

"Very well, Ann." Mrs. March's voice was brittle. "Get in, then. I just don't understand you at all."

"I doubt if you ever will understand me again, Mother!"

"What has happened to you, darling? You sound like an utter stranger to me."

"Perhaps I am! I hope I am!"

"Oh, my baby! I know you're going to break your mother's heart, if you keep up this terrible talk!"

"Sometimes, Mother, a broken heart may be a wonderful thing!"

At Frances March's home Ann hurried immediately to her room. She sat on the edge of the bed, her mind working vigorously. A memory stabbed her deeply. Paul had stood in the pulpit, giving one of his sermons. He had said, "Someone asked the Devil what he missed most in heaven and he said, 'Most of all I miss the trumpets in the morning!'

Nothing can ever take the place of the trumpets blowing in the soul! Calling the soul on higher, toward Home. That's why some of us must keep on, no matter what the cost, with the Gospel of Christ. We have to keep hearing the trumpets of God sound!"

Ann sank down on her knees.

"Dear God, what can I say to Paul, to my husband — whom I forsook when he needed me so? Will he believe me, after I've hurt him so? I'll say to him, sweetheart, I am a traitor, a coward and quitter! Can you find it possible to forgive me in your heart? Oh, let me come home to you, my darling, where I belong, where I've always belonged, and I'll make it up to you, somehow . . . I'll stand and fight for you till I can stand up no longer. . . ."

She sprang up and grabbed a suitcase and began tossing things into it.

"*Ann!*"

Her mother's voice downstairs was something of a shriek. "Hurry! Come here — "

Ann ran down the stairs. "What is it?"

"It's on television! A tornado! Oklahoma — !"

Ann sprang toward the television set. A voice came out of it. "— a tornado struck the earth at Sheola, Oklahoma, a few minutes ago, doing untold damage, and taking many lives —"

"Oh, no!" cried Ann. "Oh, no — *no!* Not Sheola —!"

CHAPTER 25

PAUL SAT IN HIS STUDY. It was seven o'clock on Monday evening. Cal Young was with him. There were intermittent growls of thunder. The sun had departed in a bed of angry black clouds. The air was humid and hot.

"That was a fine sermon yesterday morning, Paul," said Young.

"Thanks, Cal. I didn't think I could preach. But once I got going the Lord helped me."

"That subject hit me hard. The Cross. Sometimes I wonder if we have forgotten what it means. We want cushions, ease, riches. And Jesus had a crown of thorns!"

"Uh-huh. We quote the text, 'We are heirs, and joint-heirs, with Christ.' But we forget the rest of the text! 'If so be that we *suffer* with Him!'"

"Some of us are grasping what it means to be a Christian in this town. Thanks to your ministry."

"Thanks. Will I be able to stay on here? With Ann gone, I mean? There'll be so many questions — "

"You'll stay. Carla and I are with you, to the hilt!"

"God bless you both. But there are many others — "

"I saw George Rover today. He said he had heard of

your trouble. He's for you, to the finish.''

"Good old George!"

"There are others. They haven't all heard yet. But most of them will stick. You've got roots in this town deeper than you know!"

"What would I do without you, Cal?"

Young sighed. "I need help, too!"

Paul saw the trouble in his face, then. "What is it, Cal?"

"I don't like to burden you with *my* griefs — ''

"Tell me.''

"I've got one big trouble. You've heard of the Ragland Oil Company?"

"I think so."

"Well, they sold me on a big deal. I invested heavily. Seems they were playing me for a sucker! Their setup showed swell on paper; they seemed to have some fine oil prospects. I knew one guy in the outfit and had confidence in him. He was the one really that over-sold me. But he turns out to be a double-crosser. He's working for another man — a man I never dreamed was as big as he is! The man, the big man, has drawn out his capital and left me holding an empty sack! Looks like I'm ruined, or close to it!"

Paul sat staring at him. Matt had told him once that he was getting to be a big oil man —

"You mean *Matt?*" Paul cried.

Young nodded soberly. "Right."

Paul swung out of his chair. "This is terrible! Matt kept saying he'd get you — I never thought he'd have an opportunity like this!"

"He made the opportunity. But he hasn't reckoned on one thing. *God!*"

Paul nodded. "Yes. Matt will have to find out the hard way about Him! But I'm sick for you, Cal! Why must it happen to a man like you?"

"Shall we dig up that word 'why?' and kick it around?"

"I'm sorry."

"We just got through saying something about a man

being able to suffer for Christ, remember?''

Paul sat at his desk after Cal had gone, resentment burning in him against Matt. But compassion for Young rose above resentment, and he began to pray for the oil man.

At last he found himself praying for Ann. When he finished this prayer he looked at Ann's picture on the desk. Once he had removed the picture; but he had put it back. Ann was smiling at him in the picture. He thought of how seldom she had smiled in the weeks before she left him.

Poor little beat-up flower! his mind said. *But I may not be blameless. In a way I did what her mother did; I over-shielded her.*

Suddenly his head snapped up. The rain had been pouring steadily for the last few minutes, but now it slackened, and he heard a louder sound. Then abruptly the rain stopped, and terrifyingly clear came that other sound.

CHAPTER 26

PAUL WAS HALF-WAY TO THE DOOR when the approaching noise sent him wheeling back toward his desk. He felt the church shudder from roof to basement, heard the sound of a hundred wrecking crews; he flung himself under the desk. Crouched there he heard the church come apart, heard thunder in his ears. An avalanche of stone and bricks roared like cataracts. The desk shivered above him, but stayed in place. A piece of flying brick struck him over the right eye and he was stunned.

When consciousness rushed back he felt the sticky blood trying to close his eye. He wiped it away and stirred amid the ruin. The tornado had left the church a mountain of rubble; he heard the storm in the distance, raging dreadfully.

He dragged himself out from under the desk. The study was gone; he bruised himself in the darkness, cut his hands on sharp debris. Then he remembered there was a large flashlight in one of the drawers of the desk. He found a beam wedged against the drawer, but managed to move it enough to get the flashlight. He switched it on and stood gaping at the mountainous rubble flung up about him.

A message flashed to his brain. *Nonna!*

He clambered through the debris, seeking the sidewalk, wondering if he could find Nonna's house in the ruin. He prayed, too, that Nonna was safe. Her house was several blocks away; he began struggling toward it.

In the light of the flash he saw a car that had been wadded as a ball of tinfoil in a giant's fingers. Trees that had lined a familiar street were gone. Some were uprooted as weeds that are pulled. Some were carried clean away. A few remained, their branches turned to naked slivers. Buildings that had stood making a familiar skyline were also gone. Sheola was an open field, now, a field of ruin.

Paul struggled on, remembering things he had heard about tornadoes. A tornado is a devil sweeping the earth, leaving it full of dying and death. It may, at its greatest whirling speed, exert five hundred pound pressure on every square foot of surface which it contacts.

CHAPTER 27

MATT JENNER'S HOUSE WAS OUTSIDE the tornado path. He was wakened by the fearsome noise of the storm, feeling the house tremble from the wind-force.

He heard his wife's scream. "Tornado! Matt — a tornado!"

Matt jerked his trousers on in the darkness. He tried the light switch; there was no light. He rushed to the kitchen after a flashlight. He went out of the house, with Phyllis following him.

"Stay here!" he ordered. "I've got to see about Nonna!"

"I'm scared to stay!" cried Phyllis.

"You're safe here."

He ran to the garage and backed his car out, hurling it up the street. But he soon reached the first barricade of debris. He leaped out, leaving the headlights on. He scrambled through wreckage, falling once, slashing a forearm. He turned the light and saw the bright red seeping through the torn sleeve. He lunged on, breathing hard, fighting his way toward the street where Nonna lived. He heard cries for help and groans, but he could think only of Nonna.

After what seemed weeks he finally came to where her house had stood; and it was demolished. A moan came out of him as he stumbled forward. He was almost to the place where the house had been when he saw a figure stumble out of the ruin. His light focused on Nonna's face.

"It's Matt, Nonna!" he cried.

"Oh, Matt! Hurry — !"

"Are you all right, Nonna?" Blood ran down her face, her night-dress was torn.

"I'm all right. But he's under a big beam — "

"Who?"

"Please help me, Matt! He helped me — I was caught in the wreckage — and another beam came down on him!"

She ran back into the ruin. Matt ran after her. In what had been a hallway he put a light on Cal Young. The latter writhed under a stack of twisted timbers. He was in a half-sitting position, trapped solidly in the material.

"He was trying to get me out!" Nonna wept.

Matt stared down at his enemy's face, blood-washed in the glare of the light. Young shut his eyes. One arm was a gory thing, pinned against a piece of broken wall.

Matt thought, *This is as it should be! This was how Cal Young should come to his end! Trapped, like a dog!* Young was dying, he felt sure of that. Death was in the oil man's face.

"Please, Matt! Help me!" Nonna was down on her knees, trying to dislodge a piece of timber.

There was another flash of light behind them; and Paul came through the wreckage. He put his beam on Young.

"Hold this!" He handed the beam to Matt. He sank down beside Nonna.

"Paul!" Young's voice was shaky and hoarse. "Don't try it! It's useless. I have but a few minutes!"

"Hold on," cried Paul. "We'll get you out."

"No, Paul. You couldn't move me. Listen . . . just know God is . . . with me . . . not alone . . . God with me —" The voice stopped. The face of Cal Young was a dead man's face.

"Oh, no!" Nonna cried. "He died — trying to save me — "

Paul reached and touched Young's body. From a tortured throat he said, "You were one of the finest Christians I ever knew!" He raised his face toward Matt, tears flowing down to meet dried blood.

"He loved me!" moaned Nonna. She began to sob.

Paul stood up. Matt gazed down on the dead man, the light still focused on the still face.

As if talking to himself Matt muttered, "I tried to destroy him — !"

"Yes!" cried Paul. "A man like that!"

"How wonderful he was!" sobbed Nonna.

Matt kept looking at the dead man. He turned toward Paul. "What . . . what can I do?" he asked helplessly.

"You can ask God to have mercy on you!" He paused, added, "If Cal were alive I'm sure he'd forgive you, even as he did while he lived. Men like Cal are hard to come by!"

Nonna had her head down, praying.

Paul said, "This town is blown away. We've got to see what we can do. Will you be all right, Nonna?"

"Yes," said Nonna. "I'll do what I can, too."

Paul flung about and began working his way through the darkness. Matt stood a moment, his face twisting. Then he handed his flash, to Nonna.

"You'll need this, Nonna."

He went into the darkness, following Paul's light. "Wait, Paul. I want to help, too."

CHAPTER 28

THE DAWN REACHED BRIGHT over the ruin that had been
Sheola. Highway police cars prowled amid the ruins, sirens
growling. Tents had been set up for temporary hospitals. The
towns around Sheola had helped in every possible way.

Paul lifted a cup of black coffee in a paper cup to his
mouth. His hand shook a little. A vast weariness was in him,
pain spiraled up in his whole body. Matt stood beside him,
also sipping coffee.

The night through which they had passed was burned
into their minds. Together, through the hours, they had
worked dragging injured men, women and children from the
shattered buildings.

Paul had just finished his coffee when he saw Carla.

"I've looked and looked for you!" she said. "The
church is gone. So is the manse."

"I know, Carla," he said. "I was in the church when it
went."

"Thank God, you're safe!"

"And you, Carla."

"You're ready to drop, Paul. You must get some rest!"

"There are times when you can't rest, Carla."

"You're so tired!"

"How about you? Can you still help?"

"Yes!"

"Let's go, then."

The day seemed endless to Paul as he went on, with Matt and Carla, doing what they could for those who suffered most. Somewhere in the rubble he ran into Rover.

"There'll be a lot of funerals, Reverend," said Rover. "Looks like the end of the world, doesn't it?"

"It's another beginning," muttered Paul.

"Have you seen Cal Young?"

Paul nodded gloomily. "He's dead, George."

"Dead? Not him!"

"Yes."

Rover ran a hand over a fatigue-marred face. "Things won't ever be the same with him gone."

"No, never." Paul started to move on and Rover touched his arm. "Maybe I should tell you. Before the storm hit I had a call from Cal."

"Oh?"

"Remember the man I assigned him to check, in our cell setup?"

"I think so."

"Cal checked him out, found his need, worked on him. The fellow phoned Cal last night that he had decided to become a Christian. Cal phoned me to report. Then came the storm."

A slow smile crossed Paul's weary, blood-marked features. "A real gospel man, right to the end!"

Near the ruin of the church Paul found Nonna. She was also worn out. Her eyes were red from weeping; and he knew she was thinking of Cal Young. A huge ache was in his own heart because of Young's death.

He reeled, stumbled, went down; darkness lashed at his brain. He did not know how long the darkness held him. When he lifted from it he saw the drawn face of his wife.

"Ann!"

Her face was dirty; she was crying. She bent down and kissed him, lifting his head up to her.

"Paul, oh, Paul, my dearest!"

He tried to smile, he wanted to ask questions; but darkness tormented him again. His eyes refused to remain open. He felt Ann lift his head and lay it gently in her lap. He heard her praying; also he heard Nonna. He felt like having a long sleep. But he opened his eyes with an effort.

" — glad you came, darling — "

"Oh, Paul! When I heard the tornado had struck Sheola my heart quit! I flew down to Tulsa and got a man to drive me here. I lived an eternity before I saw you!"

He managed a small grin. "You're beautiful!"

"I'm a quitter, a traitor! Can you ever forgive me?"

"You're wonderful!" He closed his eyes.

When he opened them again Ann kissed him. Her fingertips caressed his blood-soiled face. He turned his head in her lap and saw the leveled town of Sheola.

"It's dreadful!" Ann said in a low voice.

He said, "They'll build it again. People always build again. They're like that!"

Ann looked at the rubbish-stack that had been Christ Church. "We'll build it again, too, won't we?"

"Yes."

Nonna, sitting close by, gazing upward, cried, "Look!"

Paul's eyes came to the target of her pointing finger. It was the archway of the church, which still stood, above the ruin, naked against the sky.

"Look!" Nonna repeated.

"The words on the arch!" cried Ann.

Paul looked. He had forgotten the words were up there, carved in the stone, though he had seen them many times. Now they stood clear in the sunlight, challenging and comforting.

THE WORD OF THE LORD ENDURETH FOREVER

After a time Nonna said softly, "When we build it

again, it would be nice to call it the Young Memorial Church."

Paul moved his head on Ann's lap. "Cal wouldn't like that. He'd want to keep the old name. Christ Church."

Nonna assented with her head. "He would, wouldn't he?"